Killer

CLARISSA WILD

ISBN: 151192232X
ISBN-13: 978-1511922326

CLARISSA WILD

CONTENTS

KILLER PLAYLIST

"I'd Love to Change the World" by Jetta
"Everybody Wants to Rule The World" by LORDE
"I come with Knives" by IAMX
"Happy Together" by SPiN
"Pretty When You Cry" by VAST
"Nostalghia" by Homeostasis
"Symmetry – THE HUNT" by Johnny Jewel & Nat Walker
"One Way Or Another" by Until The Ribbon Breaks

DEDICATION

This is for the people who seek righteousness and justice in the world. You won't find it here.

PROLOGUE

VANESSA

Never in my life did I think I would be the prime suspect in my husband's murder. But looking back at the choices I made, it's not so strange that people think I'm a killer.

I'm not as innocent as I portray myself. Looks can be deceiving.

However, I won't go down for this. Not when I don't deserve it.

I should've known it would end up this way. That man … Phoenix Sullivan … The moment I saw that deadly gaze in his eyes and the dark way he looked at me, I knew I was in trouble.

Big trouble.

And something tells me there's more where that

came from.

This game of catch won't be ending anytime soon.

***

PHOENIX

Look at her, in her fancy white dress, with her fake blond curls, and that sweet, deliciously fake smile. Don't you just want to fuck that pretentious smile off her face? I do. And I will.

She had no idea what was coming for her until it was too late.

You see, I'm not a nice person. When I have my eyes set on something, I do it. In this case, it was killing her husband. She probably didn't like it, but that's not my problem. She's not my target … and she'd better not turn herself into one.

I had a purpose, and nothing stands between my goal and me. Not even a pretty girl with an ass worth fucking. Nobody stands in my way, and if they do, they die.

Too bad for her, I'm like a fucking cannon. When I shoot, shrapnel flies everywhere. If she is caught in the crossfire, that's on her.

When I want something, I'm going to get it, no matter the price. Whether it's killing someone or fucking her. I had my cake and ate it all … and damn, it tasted sweet.

She wants justice; I'll give her justice … my justice.

I bet she isn't willing to pay the price.

Too bad for her, I always win.

CHAPTER 1

PHOENIX

Tonight's the perfect night to kill.

I can feel it in my veins; that undeniable urge that flows through me on nights like these. Exciting like drugs; the murderous kind.

Clouds prevent the moonlight from bursting through and cover the land in perpetual darkness. There are plenty of lanterns lighting the road ahead, but not the alley where I'm headed. In front of me is a small puddle of water, so I walk past the side to avoid splashing my new leather shoes. You see, I just bought these, and I prefer to keep them clean for as long as possible. They will probably lose their shine after tonight's killings.

Oh well, it's not like I'll need these shoes for

anything other than entering the party ahead and pretending like I belong. Gotta be fancy enough for the big crowd because, of course, someone in dirty jeans couldn't be nearly important enough as someone in a suit.

A bunch of fake fuckers. If I could, I'd burn the whole fucking place to the ground, but I'd rather not end up in jail if I can avoid it. Killing has to be done as inconspicuous as possible, so nobody knows I did it until I've already disappeared.

It's my thing; it's what I do, or rather what I've become. After all these years, I don't even remember what it was like not to be a murderer. Not that I want to remember—hell, I prefer this life to any other. Especially over the lives of those people in that party who are about to witness death.

I have to admit, it's a rush. I just love killing, especially when it's for the right reasons. Those reasons are obviously always to benefit me. Why else would I fucking murder people if not for my own pleasure? And for the money that sustains me, of course.

What can I say? I'm the scum of the earth, the disgusting vile that creeps in the corners to jump you at night … and I don't for a second regret being like this.

I turn into the alley and come face to face with a bulking, barely-fitting-in-his-suit bodyguard. I cock my head as he frowns at me, probably wondering what I'm doing here.

"Excuse me, you can't come in here," he says as I

walk closer.

I smile. "Why not? This is where the party is."

He folds his arms, making himself seem larger, but all it does for me is make it more laughable. "This is the rear entrance. If you want access, you have to use the front door. If you have a ticket, that is ..."

He doesn't believe me? Even in my fucking fancy suit? Well, fuck him. I wanted to spare his life but questioning my slickness isn't something one can get away with.

"Oh, I have a ticket, all right," I say, narrowing my eyes. "How dare you talk to a guest like that?"

"I'm sorry, sir," he says, "but I'm not allowed to let anyone pass through this door. You'll have to go to the front entrance where they can check your ticket. Sorry."

Of course, they all think I'm not a guest because, let's face it ... I look like a guy you wouldn't want your daughter to talk to, even if it was in broad daylight in your own fucking home. With my piercings, black hair, and merciless attitude, I usually scare people to death. I have the kind of face you'd see in your nightmares ... except, when you see me in real life, you're *really* dead.

Like this guy.

"Yeah, yeah ... so, let me get this straight ..." I shuffle around, looking at the floor to distract him. "You're basically telling me that I can't walk here, even though this is a public alley, just because this isn't the 'correct' entrance to the party I'm supposed to be attending?"

"I'm only doing my job."

I look up at him. "So am I."

In a fraction of a second, I've grabbed his coat and flipped it over his head. I twist around, to his back, and wrap it around his neck. The fabric stuffed in his mouth quickly muffles his screams, choking him as I drag him back into the corner of the alley. He claws at the coat, desperate to free himself before time runs out. Stumbling backward, we fall to the ground, and I wrap my legs around his chest to prevent him from moving. His body fights for survival; his legs thrash and his hands punch the air. It's no use. I will win this fight, as I always do. His energy is waning fast, and his muscles are burning through their adrenaline. It won't be long now. With his fingers growing whiter every second, all the blood is rushing to his face, in a last attempt to breathe. But it's already too late; there is no oxygen left and his lungs are shutting down.

His legs stop moving and his hands drop to the ground, the last groan slipping off his tongue like a ghost leaving his body.

Death has made his entry.

It's done.

I unwrap the coat from his face and crawl out from underneath him. Then I drag his body to the fire escape in the back and put his body just below it. I take his coat off his dead body and swing it around until it's long and thin, like a rope. Then I throw it around the bars of the fire escape, tie it, and tightly wrap the other end around his neck. I make sure his body is positioned right and the tension on the coat is just right, so that when the paramedics or police find him they'll think exactly what I want them to think; that this was a mindless suicide with no further need to investigate.

Hopefully, they won't find him before morning, and I'll be long gone.

Before I leave, I fish in his pockets and take out a rather convenient card that will grant me access to the back door of the building. Smiling at him, I say, "Sorry, dude. Business is business. No hard feelings."

***

VANESSA

One look, a simple glance, can change everything.

A nod, narrowing eyes, or a twitch of the lips is all it takes to convey a message that destroys everything.

I should've trusted my instincts, should've listened to the warning signs. The hairs on the back of my neck stand up, the dread rippling through my veins, telling me this wasn't right.

Instead, I give my husband the glass, my smile, and a soft pat on the shoulder.

"Here you go, darling," I say, giving him a peck on the cheek.

When I turn to look back at the man I exchanged looks with, he's gone.

My husband laughs and takes the glass from my hand, pulling me from my thoughts. "Vanessa, let me introduce you to Cordelia."

The woman next to him holds out her hand, her smile full of fakery as she says, "Cordelia, I'm a fan of your husband's work."

"Vanessa, lovely to meet you. My husband seems to have many fans at this party." I laugh and smile like the good wife, pretending not to have noticed the wink she gave him. Her tightly squeezed dress reminds me of my husband's hand, which was on her ass just seconds ago. I wonder if the squeeze was good enough, or if he'll find more asses to pat later.

In one go, I chug back my drink.

Everybody looks at me like I've gone insane, but I ignore them. I place my glass down on a tray held by a waiter passing by and return with a smile. "So, Cordelia, I've heard a lot about you. You're one of the actresses in my husband's movies if I'm not mistaken."

"Yes, our latest movie will be airing in January this year, so I'm quite excited about that."

"Oh, that's wonderful. Did you work closely with her?" I ask my husband. "Since you two seem to know each other so well."

"Ah, yes, well ..." My husband chokes on his wine.

"Phillip showed me all around the set. He's quite a charmer," she says, giggling. "He knows so much about this business. I swear that I feel like a rookie again when I'm around him."

"Hmm … I can imagine," I say, smiling again. First name basis already. That went quickly.

Phillip coughs a couple more times, his wine glass shaking so much that it spills and droplets fall to the ground.

"Oh dear, are you all right, Phillip?" Cordelia asks, placing her hand on her chest.

He coughs some more, this time bending over, punching his own chest. I grab the glass from his hand and put it down. "Phillip? Talk to me," I say.

"I'm … fine," he mutters, but I can clearly tell he's not. He's coughing too much, more than I've ever seen him do, and that's noteworthy, as he's a fervent smoker.

"Do you need me to help you?" I ask.

"No … no, no, I just need some air."

I place my hand on his back. "Let's go outside then."

"I think it's better if you took him home," Cordelia says, swallowing away the lump in her throat. "He seems … ill."

"Thank you for your concern," I say. Always so involved. "We'll be fine."

"No, she's right." Phillip places a hand on mine. "Let's go home. Seems this wine was a little too much for my body to handle. I've had enough drinks for one night." He laughs, but it's more pathetic than anything else. "Besides, I've shown my face and talked to some people. The party will probably go on fine without us."

"All right, if you're sure. See you later, Cordelia," I say, waving back at her while I take my husband outside.

The doors are opened for us as I escort him outside. My husband dismisses all the help the waiters want to give him, much to my dismay. I help him down the stone staircase, which is quite a feat. The more we walk, the more he leans on me, and it's becoming harder and harder to help him walk. Soon, I'm the one carrying most of his weight.

"What's happening to you? Are you okay?"

"I'm fine," he says, the coughs still increasing in volume. "Just had a little too much, that's all." He stumbles across the pavement, almost pulling me down with him. I can barely keep us both on two feet.

"Phillip, this isn't right. You can't even walk," I say, walking him all the way to our car.

"Nothing's wrong, I'm just a little … tipsy, that's all." He fumbles in his pockets, leaning against the car as he takes his keys out and I open the door to step in.

"No, no, I'm driving," he says.

"What? No way, you can't. You're too intoxicated."

He frowns. "No, I'm not. Now, step aside and let me drive."

I make a face. "Must you always be so damn

stubborn? Just let me drive. I can get us home safely."

"There's nothing wrong. Now move aside, woman." He shoves me so hard that I have to hold onto the door to stay steady.

Before I have time to protest, he sits down behind the wheel and slams the door shut.

My hands turn into fists as I storm to the other side of the car and mouth some foul words. This man ... ugh, the amount of crap I have to put up with is driving me insane.

I open the door and sit my ass down, slamming the door shut behind me. The car starts and he drives off with a hiccup, hitting a stone ridge to the side of the road.

"Watch it!" I say.

"Oh, c'mon," he says, driving out of the parking lot. "Can you just give me a break?"

"No, this is dangerous, and you know it."

"I said I'm fine. What more do you want from me, huh?" He starts driving faster.

"Oh, not this again," I sigh.

"Keep quiet then and let me do my job."

"Your job is driving?" I jest, as we ride through the city.

He throws me a glance. "Can you just not make it worse? Like, for one fucking second in my life, can you just not annoy the ever-loving shit out of me?"

The car is going faster and faster, even when a traffic light is eminent.

"Phillip, stop."

"No, you stop."

"No, I mean, the lights!" I yell.

Too late, he's already rushing straight through after it had turned red. I put my hands in front of my eyes so I won't see the impending disaster. My heart is racing, my breathing is ragged, and when I open my eyes, again nothing has happened. Phillip is still sitting next to me; his breathing is loud and his veins bulge through his skin, his face red with rage.

"What in the *hell* is wrong with you?" I scream.

"Nothing, you're what's wrong with me!" he yells back.

"You just drove straight through a red light. Are you insane?"

"If I am, it's your fucking fault for always getting on my back," he hisses.

"And this is payback? Scaring me? How dare you," I say. "Stop this car."

"No."

We're nearing the highway, and I don't want this to get worse. I need to get out. "Phillip, stop this car. Right. Now."

"No," he repeats, fuming.

"Let me out!" I scream.

"We're not doing this. Not now," he says, gritting his teeth.

I look around, but all I see are roads and other cars; no grass in sight to even remotely think of jumping out, even though that's a ridiculous idea. But when you're afraid, stupid things go through your head. I hate danger.

Shit, we're already driving on the highway. It's too late.

"What are you doing?" I ask. "Get off the highway!"

"I'm driving us home. Now will you shut up already?" he yells. "You're driving me crazy with your constant whining."

The yelling causes him to cough so hard, the car swerves.

"Be careful," I say, sweating like crazy.

"Shut up! Just shut up, all right? If you can shut your mouth for like ten minutes, we'll get home safely, and I'll be rid of this nasty cough," he growls, still coughing.

"Fine," I say, and I turn my head to look out the window.

The lights pass by quicker with every mile we drive, cars shooting by as if they were never even there. I try to focus on my breathing, trying to calm myself down so I can think of a rational solution to this problem. The problem being his cough and incredibly bad temper. I try to ignore the fact that the car is still speeding up and that his cough still has not subsided, even though he said it would when we'd stop talking. After a few minutes, the swaying becomes so bad that I turn my head to see if I can help.

What I see makes my heart stop.

Phillip's eyes open and close.

His body is limp.

His hands aren't on the steering wheel.

And the car has already veered from one lane into the other.

"No!" I squeal, grasping the wheel with all I have, trying to straighten it in time.

But the car is already too skewed, and when I turn the wheel, it starts to spin.

The backside slips to the left, crashing into the guardrail. Another car hits ours so hard it catapults us into the air.

At this moment in time, my body is bumping into my seat and my head into the window, exploding in pain. My vision becomes blurry as the car cartwheels across the road. I swing from left to right, up and down, as the belt proves to be of little use to protect me. My hands clamp around my face in an attempt to protect myself as the car flips again and again.

When the car comes to a stop, I'm hanging from the top and gravity is pulling on my body. My lungs are about to burst from the air locked inside. For a moment, my mind leaves my body, and I fade in and out of consciousness. Blood trickles down my nose, keeping me awake. My hands feel numb and my feet are swollen, but somewhere inside me, I find the courage to move.

I lift the belt and unbuckle myself. My body drops

to the hard roof, which is now the floor, crushing my ribs. I howl in pain, but stop when I can't breathe. I blink to clear my view and look around. Phillip hangs next to me, his body lifeless and limp. And then I notice the smoke.

"Phillip," I whisper. "Phillip, wake up." My throat burns and my muscles ache as I attempt to free him. However, a flicker of fire is enough to make me stop in my tracks. Flames are eating up the car, and by the time I slide out of the car, they have swallowed the metal.

I crawl further away, hoping to get on my feet and run to Phillip's side so I can drag him out myself, but when I try to stand, my legs won't budge. Cars around us stop as I fight to get away from the car. The fuel entering my nostrils is the adrenaline that pushes me to keep going.

When I turn my head to look at the car, flames have engulfed it.

My ears are ringing, my eyes tearing up from the pain.

My husband is in there, and despite my efforts, I can't make it back in time.

He's burning alive.

"No!" I yell but then cough because I can't bear the pain. It's so hot, and everything hurts.

As I look around, someone comes toward me. One of the people from the cars that stopped. My vision is getting blurry again, and my strength is fading fast. Even though I try to lift my arms, they don't listen to me, and I lie lifelessly on the cold asphalt, waiting for the ordeal to end.

Feet come closer until they stop in front of me. I pour my last ounce of strength into gazing up into the eyes of the one who will pull me out of here.

He's none other than the man at the party.

But his eyes show no mercy.

CHAPTER 2

PHOENIX

A few minutes ago

The moment they step into the car, I rush through the back entrance and run to my own car. I would've stopped her from going with him if it weren't for the fact that the place was crowded. Why the fuck did they leave anyway? He was supposed to collapse on the floor, or in the fucking bathroom, but not drive his fucking car.

I jump in my Audi A8, start it up, and race off the parking lot. Trailing behind them, I make sure they don't see me as they drive to the highway. I wonder what he's planning to do, but he won't go far. I doubt they'll even make it home. The chain reaction has already been set into motion, and once he passes out, the car will steer out of control. I can already see it coming miles ahead. Nothing will save them.

It's unfortunate that she had to step into the car with him, but I can't change the past. I dislike unnecessary casualties, but if it happens, so be it.

I watch as the car starts to swerve and then the spinning begins. The car hits the rails and I slow down as it catapults onto the asphalt road, tumbling over. Once it comes to a stop, the metal is already set ablaze.

I stop my car not far ahead of the accident. Other cars slow down around us, but I'm the first to block the road. The fire crackles as I step out of my car and look at the onslaught. It wasn't supposed to end up this way, but at least I can be sure he's dead now.

I walk toward the wreckage where the girl comes crawling out, barely conscious. Noise comes from her mouth as she wriggles across the ground toward me. She looks up to gaze at me before her head drops on the ground.

Cocking my head to look at her, I fish in my pocket, whip out my phone, and dial the number.

"It's done," I say.

I close the phone immediately and go to my knees. My fingers instinctively reach for her face as I wipe away the dirt and blackened hairs. She's beautiful. A beautiful, wretched, ruined girl.

I didn't mean to drag her into this, but I guess she had it coming for her.

If you associate yourself with men like him, you're

going to be in trouble.

However, some part of me feels a little taken aback watching her die slowly on the cold, hard ground. My heart, which rarely beats for anyone, tugs at me for some reason and I can't shake it off. I should feel nothing; no remorse, no guilt, no sorrow, no anger … nothing. But this woman …

Sighing, I pick up her limp body and drag her further away from the car, which flames have engulfed. I pull her all the way off to the side of the road as onlookers flock to the fire.

"I'm being nice now," I say, as I place her in the bushes where it's safe. "I normally don't do this, but I'll make an exception for you. Once." I know I'm talking to a passed out person, but I don't care.

I take out my phone again. "I'd like to report a car accident."

***

VANESSA

The light shining down upon me blinds me. I blink a couple of times, wondering if this is the tunnel they speak about, and if I'm about to walk into heaven. Would it look like the place in my dreams? Coconut trees, white sandy beaches, a scorching sun, an endless ocean, and all the men in the world at my feet begging to touch just an inch of my skin...

I don't remember falling asleep. My body just wouldn't move, and now ... now it feels like I'm floating. Floating through the air, drifting on an endless stream of subconscious thoughts. I'm not sure where I am, but that's all right. Anywhere is better than on that highway. In that car. Burning.

I shudder, and somehow, it prickles on my skin. Am I supposed to feel something in heaven? I don't know. Am I even there? Is that light really a tunnel? I don't remember dying ... just darkness and pain. A lot of pain.

It hurts to try to move. The bedding is soft, but my body aches with every tightening of my muscles. My eyes start burning, and I get the urge to rub them. Only after a little while do my hands actually move to my face. It's then that I realize there are wires in the way.

This can't be heaven. It wouldn't pin me down like this. Pain should not exist here. I refuse to accept that.

After focusing intensely, just like during a bad nightmare I want to wake up from, my eyes manage to open. The light was neither a tunnel nor heaven. It's a bright fluorescent light on the ceiling. A soft beep is audible. For a moment, I believe I'm on a stage and there are people near me cheering me on. The story has ended. The woman died. Applause ensues.

But not everything is a play.

This isn't heaven, where I get to act out every

fantasy I ever had.

This is real life, and I'm still alive, breathing in this hell.

A painful hell.

My lungs hurt each time they suck in the oxygen to breathe. My eyes search to find something meaningful, but all they find are humans dressed in white coats, holding charts in their hands. The beep is getting louder and louder until the sound becomes so annoying, I want to scream, even though I can't.

My mouth is dry, my lips raw, and the only noise coming from me sounds like a bird being choked to death.

"Where am I?" I ask the man nearby. At least, I think it is a man.

The blur that walks to me turns into a person with quite a distinctive beard. I knew it was a man.

"You're in the hospital," he says.

His voice is muffled, like mine, as if there are cloths over our mouths meant to slowly strangle us. Silence is the best tool to shut someone up, however, now it feels like my mind is silencing me instead. Something wants to come out ... something important. A memory, perhaps. Something flaring and evil.

Eyes.

I gasp and shoot up from the bed, all beeps going off like crazy.

"It's him!" I yell with a raspy voice.

The doctor pushes me down. "Mrs. Starr! You'll

hurt yourself."

My breathing is erratic, and my heart is almost beating out of my chest just because of that vision inside my head. I saw him; that man, his conniving eyes, and that devilish smirk on his face.

"I saw him," I repeat, voicing the thoughts going on in my head.

"Who? What are you talking about?" The doctor keeps me down on the bed. "Mrs. Starr, you have to lie down or your stitches will spring."

"Stitches?" I ask.

"Yes, you were hurt quite badly from the crash."

"Crash?" I keep repeating his words because I don't understand. I can't think of anything else but those eyes … those eyes haunt me.

The doctor sighs. "Please lie down, Mrs. Starr, and try to get some rest. You're still healing, and you need all the energy you can muster."

"But I have to tell them …" I mumble, my eyes still droopy. I can't keep them open.

"Tell who what?"

My mouth opens, but my vocal cords won't budge. I can't say it, and I've already forgotten half of what I was going to say. Why is my head so cloudy?

"Just go to sleep. We'll talk some more when you wake up," he says, smiling. "Rest assured, we will do our very best to care for you."

"Thank you," I croak, not even remembering what he just said.

I still feel so sleepy. So drowsy …

It doesn't take long before I black out again.

***

When I wake up again, there is someone at my bed.

Arthur, Phillip's younger and certainly more attractive brother. They look very much alike, except Arthur kept all the charming bits that his brother, Phillip, lost over the years. That, and he clearly takes better care of his physique.

For a moment, I wonder why he's here. Although, we've always had a strong bond and it would make sense for him to come to my side in the hospital. I wouldn't have expected him to be the first to visit. Even after all these years, his devotion to me is untouched.

His eyes are glossy the moment he sees me look at him.

"Hi," I say, giving him a tiny smile.

"Vanessa, you're awake," he says. "How are you feeling?"

"Better … I think."

He smiles, but it's no genuine smile. Frowning, he drops his head. "Did the doctors tell you anything?"

"No?" I ask. As I sit up, it hurts my body, but I manage to do it without the help he offers. "What should they have told me?"

"Do you remember what happened to you?" he

asks.

"A little ..." My brain crunches. "I was in an accident, wasn't I?"

"Yes," Arthur says, running his fingers through his hair. "You're lucky you're still alive."

I swallow away the lump in my throat, not knowing how to respond to that. I don't want to imagine escaping death by an inch, but I do. Memories flash through my head—the party, having a drink, and then leaving with the car ... the highway ... the car tumbling around, spinning through the air. Phillip.

"Where's Phillip?" I quickly ask, holding my breath.

Arthur mulls around as if he's afraid to speak the words. He fumbles with his shirt and licks his lips. "He ... he didn't make it."

My jaw drops, my lips shuddering. My body shakes, and it feels like even my bones are trembling. "He's ... dead ..." I mumble, unsure how in the hell it all happened. I can't believe it ... and yet, it did. Phillip is dead. My husband is dead.

Oh, my god.

I gaze at Arthur who immediately grabs my hand and holds it, gently caressing it. "I'm sorry."

"You're sorry?" I stammer. "He's *your* brother."

"He is—was, yes, but he was your husband."

"I can't believe he's actually dead. He's really gone?"

"Yes. They were too late to ... get him out of the burning car."

My lips part, but nothing comes out. I have difficulty coming to terms with what happened, but also with my own emotions because honestly … I don't feel anything. It's all blank.

It's quiet for some time. I guess neither of us knows what to say. Nothing can be said that can make this any better to deal with, and I know that he feels the same way.

"It's going to be okay," he says.

He comes closer and opens his arms. I gently slide into his arms, letting him wrap them around me. His hug makes me sigh as I rest my head on his shoulder and look at the clock ticking on the wall. The time has stopped, but only for us, not for the outside world.

"I don't know what to say," I mumble. It's the truth.

All I can think about is the burning corpse inside that car.

The images make my heart lose control. I never expected Phillip to die that way.

"You don't have to say anything. It's okay if you want to cry," he says. "You have my shoulder." His warm hand comforts me and makes me feel safe.

"Thank you …" I say. "I just don't know if I want to cry."

"Take your time," he says. "I'm here for you."

He leans back and looks at me, smiling gently. Deeply seated affection fills his eyes. "I'm not going anywhere. I'll stay here every day if you need me." He places his hand on my cheek and caresses it. It feels genuine but so wrong at the same time.

"But what about you?" I grab his hand. "He's your brother. You need someone just as much."

"I can handle it," he says. "Don't worry about me. Worry about your own health." He leans in and presses a kiss to my forehead. "You should get some rest."

When he gets up, I reach for his wrist. "Don't go."

He looks back. "I don't want to be here if your parents come. It wouldn't be … right." The way he says it confirms my suspicions, and it flatters me, even though it shouldn't.

We've always connected on a level Phillip and I couldn't, which is why this feels so bad … but I need it more than anything in the world right now.

Phillip isn't here. I have no one else to keep me company. I need Arthur as much as he needs me right now.

"Stay with me," I say. "I don't mind."

"But your parents—"

"Let them talk," I interrupt. "I don't care."

I smile at him, and I can see him changing his mind.

So he sits down beside me in his chair and holds my hand, while we exchange tender, compassionate looks.

Hard times call for desperate measures.

And we're both in desperate need of consolation. In whatever way necessary.

CHAPTER 3

VANESSA

A few days later …

When the doctor comes to my bed, I'm already wide awake. I demanded his presence because I'm tired of being forced to stay in this bed. I lift my gown like always and show him the scar on my hip, which healed quite nicely with the stitches, and the cuts on my arms and belly have almost disappeared. I'm so lucky my face was spared. Just a few bruises here and there and a swollen lip, but nothing too bad.

I've not yet looked in the mirror. All the things I know, the female nurses have told me. The men … well, they don't prove to be of much use. All they say is how healthy I look compared to the day before. Some even call me pretty. I think they're just interested in buying the meat that just got onto the market.

Tsk. As if I'd ever allow that to happen.

I like my men like I like my wine; powerful and overtaking. Of course, flirting and casual sex are great, but nothing that involves more than a one-time kind of thing. Besides, it's not like that's going to work, with me being in a hospital. I have other things on my mind right now, like my dead husband, for example.

To flirt with a guy now wouldn't be … kosher.

"Looking good, Mrs. Starr," the doctor says.

"Oh, call me Vanessa already. Let's drop the pretenses." I chuckle to lighten my words.

He nods. "Your wounds have healed quite nicely; I'd say you'll be out of here in a couple of days."

"A couple of days? But it's already been a couple of days. I feel fine."

"I'd prefer not to take the risk, so just to be sure, I won't discharge you yet."

I frown, sighing out loud when a man walks in who makes my eyes widen.

"Father?"

"Vanessa," he says as he comes closer and hugs me tight then lets me go again.

"Oh, darling, your father and I were so worried about you. We couldn't get here any sooner, but I was so worried about you. Give your mother a hug." My mom busts in, pushes my father aside, and wraps her arms around my neck, almost choking me.

"I'm fine, Mother."

"No, you're not, and don't you dare say that! You were in a car accident. You should be glad you're alive."

"I am," I say. "But I'm one of the more fortunate ones."

"Poor Phillip," she says, and then she sighs. "It wasn't his time yet."

"I find the accident quite unusual, however," my father says. "I never expected something like that to happen."

"Me neither. Phillip is normally a great driver." I lie to keep up the image my parents had of him. It comes easily to me. Besides, I don't want to come across as foolish for stepping into the car with him, knowing he was that intoxicated.

"Well, there must've been something wrong. Aren't they investigating it?" my mother asks. She looks directly at the doctor, as if he would know.

"Yes, I believe so," I say.

"The police have actually requested to speak with you, Mrs. Starr."

"They have?" my mother says.

The doctor clears his throat. "I told them that you weren't well enough yet."

"I am now," I say. "Do they know anything?" I'm getting anxious already.

"Yes, I would like to speak with them as well," my mother says.

"Mother!" I make a face at her. "I can handle this

myself."

"Nonsense. You're not fit enough."

"Oh, darling. Let her decide on her own," my father says, sighing. "Let's just go grab a cup of coffee."

My father drags her away from my bed, but she sputters, "Coffee? From this place? I wouldn't dare touch that gunk!"

And then they disappear through the door.

The doctor nods at me and smiles. "Not easy, huh?"

"Ugh, they bore me to death," I say. "So overprotective and not in a good way."

"They seem to care a lot about you," he muses.

"No. That's just charades. We've learned to play well," I retort.

The doctor frowns. I don't think he gets it. Nobody does. That's why our family works the way it does, why it's so successful; we are perfect liars. We shroud ourselves in an aura of compassion, love, and tenderness while plotting to kill the people around us with our bare hands. Well, maybe not literally, although I could never know. My parents are, after all, the perfect liars, even to me.

They don't love me.

They just pretend they do.

Love is just a word thrown around to make us look good, but underneath the surface, it rots.

My parents raised me in such an environment

where looks, appearance, and attitude were all that mattered, and real emotions were better kept hidden. They didn't serve the grand purpose; the quest for power.

That's what it's always been about. No matter what the subject was, whether it was getting the highest grades in high school, being at the top of the class in college, landing the best job, or marrying the richest man in town … it was always about achieving the very best. Simple satisfaction wasn't worth it, and my parents wouldn't accept anything less than perfection.

Money and power. Those are the only things that matter to them.

I am just a tool for them to acquire more power. How? With my marriage to Phillip, who they adored so much. Not because of his looks or intellect. No, because of his influence in the movie business. That, and his money, of course, which my father spends on his campaigns. Their perfect daughter married one of the biggest directors in Hollywood. Well, isn't that just perfect?

I crumple up the sheets covering my body and take a deep breath.

Even when everything seems perfect, life isn't always a fairy tale.

"Well …" the doctor murmurs, interrupting my flow of thought.

"Yes?" I ask.

Someone knocks on the door. It's the police.

"Is it all right?" they ask the doctor.

The doctor throws me a glance and then looks at them over his shoulder. "I believe so, yes." He smiles at me. "I will see you again later, Mrs. Starr."

"It's Vanessa, for next time." I throw him a wink, which makes him smile even more. Charming.

The police step in and nod at me. "Glad to see you're well, Mrs. Starr."

"Thank you," I say. "It's been quite the ordeal."

"Our condolences for your loss; it must've been terrible to wake up with that news."

I nod, unsure how to answer.

One of the officers clears his throat and grabs a notebook. "If you're okay with that, we'd like to ask you some questions."

"What for, if I may ask?"

"We just want to know what happened. Can you tell us what you remember?"

I dig into the back of my mind. Bits and pieces have come back, mostly from the party, but I don't remember everything from the actual accident. Except that Phillip was feeling ill when we drove back home, and then suddenly, I was lying on the asphalt, injured. And those eyes … those dark, soulless eyes. They bore into me like death.

"Ma'am?"

"Huh?" I shake my head. "Sorry, I was a bit lost in my thoughts."

"No worries. We'd just like to know if you saw

anything weird. Did your husband act strangely?"

"Well, he did have a nasty cough at the party," I say.

"Anything else?"

"Why are you asking?" I ask.

"We want to know every bit of detail so we can piece this together. Did you catch your husband talking about something odd or to someone you don't know?"

Ah, my husband and his infamous charm. I guess everyone knows. No point in hiding it then. He did have a thing for the ladies, and it wasn't just talking. Oh no, I wish it was just talking that I caught him doing.

***

Hours before the party

When you come home from dinner with a friend, you don't expect to find your husband in bed. Not at four in the afternoon with another woman.

I watch them through the small opening in the door. They haven't noticed me yet. I wonder if they ever will because they're so enraptured with each other. The way he fucks her, no-holds-barred, facing each other, shows an intimacy that even we don't have.

Phillip rarely fucked me, and when he did, it was always from behind. It wasn't for love. It was always just sex. Mostly for his pleasure. I just went along with it. Gotta please the husband so he's happy. At least, that's what they tell you when you marry someone. Make them happy. I think it only works if it goes both ways.

Luckily, those days are long gone.

I take off my necklace and place it on the small cabinet in the hallway. I've seen her before, that whore he brought in. She stepped into his car the other day after he left home. I saw it through the window. My husband thinks I don't know, but I'm not blind. It's good that he believes that, though. Easier to keep the fakery up.

My earrings go next as I hear her scream and moan out loud like the whore she is. I don't know her name. They come and go like cheap wine swallowed by that swine of a husband. I ponder if I should clear my throat and walk in at the moment he blows his load. Just the look on his face and the ruined orgasm would be worth the price I'd have to pay. Although, tonight wouldn't be a good night to taunt him. A big, red bruise on my face wouldn't look good at the party. Imagine what people would say.

Besides, it's not like anything I do will make him stop cheating. His sexual appetite is different from mine, and I will never be able to please him the way he desires. Nor can he please me. I like my men rough, demanding, and emotional with a strong imagination. Phillip likes his girls the way he likes directing a movie; quick, to the point, and without fuss or difficulty. I'm the opposite of what I just described. We were never a match made in heaven. However, when I agreed to marry him, I didn't think I'd be witnessing my husband loving other women more than me.

What girl in their right mind would have said yes to that?

Exactly. But I did.

Some would spur me on to divorce him. As if it was that simple. When you come from a family like mine, there is more to a marriage than love. There is an obligation. Money. Power. Deals. Agreements. Signed papers. Lawsuits. Lies.

Even death.

If I fail to uphold the vow, the world wouldn't be a small enough of a place to hide. Not from him or my parents. Not everything is as simple as it seems. There is no black and white. There are many shades of gray, and my shade is the kind that stopped believing in fairy tales, stopped living her life, and stopped breathing entirely.

Instead, I'm just a mold of the perfect wife, who ignores her husband's cheating and forgives him for bringing a whore into their home.

This home. My home. My perfect home.

It is a beautiful home, though.

I smile, sighing to myself. So happy together, living a perfect lie.

Then I turn and tiptoe down the stairs without making a sound.

We're expected at the party in a few hours. Better

make sure I look prim and proper. Time for my pedicure.

***

Present

I frown, thinking about all the things I could tell them … or not. "Well, if you consider touching someone's ass weird behavior, then yes, he might have been acting strange."

The police officers are quiet for a moment, their lips parted, and their brows furrowed. "Uh, okay. Can you tell us who it was he was flirting with?"

"Her name's Cordelia. They work together." I look straight into the eyes of the officer who's so privy to my private life. "My husband likes to cheat. He does it all the time."

Slamming their lips together, they nod slowly while one of them pens it down.

"Thank you, ma'am. Anything else you thought was particularly off about the party? Some other guests, maybe?"

I think about this for a second. If I should answer or not. Anything I say can and will be used against me. The first suspect in homicide cases is always the next of kin. And truth be told, Phillip was acting weirdly. Who knows, this whole thing might've been set up.

Someone might've wrecked the car. Or worse …

someone might have killed Phillip on purpose.

And then it dawns on me.

This might actually be the truth.

I swallow away the lump in my throat. That car crash was no accident. My husband has many enemies, which makes him an easy target. However, my biggest concern is the fact that I'm his wife, and wives are always one of the prime suspects.

Especially when the husband and wife are both cheating bastards.

CHAPTER 4

VANESSA

A few days later ...

Arthur returns to visit me, and the moment I see his face, I'm feeling much better already. Especially considering the fact that the police might question me again, and I don't want to tell them what really happened at the party.

"Hey, how are you?" he asks, as he presses a compassionate kiss to my cheek.

"Better, although I'm a bit scared," I say, as he sits down next to me.

"How come?"

"Well, I fear the police will come back to question me, and I won't know how to answer their questions."

His brows furrow. "What happened, Vanessa? Are

you sure you're okay?"

"I'm fine. It's just that I realize I can't keep everything I do hidden. Not if it means lying to the police."

"What do you have to lie about? You didn't do anything wrong," he says.

Arthur is such a gentleman, always believing in my innocence.

I'm not so sure myself.

Biting my lip, I answer, "Well, I'm not sure, to be honest. I was in a bad mood, and I did something that I might regret now."

"What? What happened?" He grabs my hand. "Is it because of him and those girls again?"

Arthur knew what a dirty pig his brother was. At first, I was afraid that telling him would mean I'd get into trouble. Luckily, it only made him hate his brother more. It also increased his infatuation with me.

"There was a ... woman in our bedroom. They were together," I say, swallowing away my nerves. "I haven't told the police."

"Is that it? That doesn't incriminate you," he says, a sigh of relief leaving his mouth.

"I wish. Except that I couldn't stomach the thought of him tumbling around with some woman in what was supposed to be *our* bed."

"I can imagine," he says.

"I was angry, Arthur. So angry." I look him directly in the eye. "I wanted him to feel just as bad. I wanted to hurt him, Arthur. I wanted revenge."

"What did you do?" he asks, frowning as if I just dug up a body.

Now is the time to tell him the truth. The reason why I'm so afraid.

Why I think it could incriminate me as my husband's murderer.

I slept with another man.

***

During the party ...

Don't mess with a scorned wife. She'll return the inflicted pain times a thousand.

On the outside, I seem calm, charming even, but on the inside, I'm boiling and ready for revenge. In my pretty dress and high heels, adorning the arm of a rich man who brings whores to his home, I join the party of equally slimy people. All for the sake of reputation. That's all that matters in a world where money is power.

But I won't sit by and let this man waltz all over my feelings.

If he doesn't care, I will make him care.

When the small talk is over, I excuse myself and walk to the bar. I need a drink before I figure out how I'm going to get what I want. The kind of guy who's a stranger to everyone, elusive but filled with unknown desires… a guy who's dangerous. Slick, combed back black hair with the sides trimmed short, black gauges in his ears, a barbell in his left eyebrow and right underneath his lip, and tattoos running from his hands all the way up to his torso. Trouble and lust, a delicious and deadly combination. Just the kind that I should avoid like the plague but need like my life depends on it. The kind that makes even the coldest of hearts catch fire.

The kind that's standing next to me right now.

I can't believe this man is here, out of all places to be. It's like a dream come true right now. A deviously bad, but oh, so good dream.

He's playing with his wallet, and on the leather, an engraved name is stamped: Phoenix Sullivan. Well, isn't that nice.

He tucks it back into his pocket in no time. With a quick glance at the mirror hanging from the wall, I check how I look, making sure my fake blond curls still look good and my red lipstick isn't smudged. Then I turn my attention toward the handsome man standing just a few inches away.

As I step closer, his eyes zoom in on me like a hawk zooming in on prey. That focus alone gives me fever.

"Hey stranger," I say, chuckling a bit.

"Hello." He picks up a glass of champagne from the bar.

"So, what brought you to this party?" I ask, putting on my flirty voice.

"I'm here to fulfill a job for a client." He takes a sip from his drink.

"Oh, really? And what kind of a job might that be?"

He looks me straight in the eyes, his face unmoving, chilling me to the bone. "Confidential."

"Oh … exciting," I joke, touching his arm.

Just that one touch is enough to tell he's buff. His muscles bulge through his black vest, and I can't imagine what else is hiding underneath that slick outfit.

"Not really," he says. "But it must be done." He takes another sip.

"Hmm … such dedication. I like it."

"Is there anything you required, Mrs.?" he suddenly asks, flashing me a quick smile that sets my body on fire.

"Just your time," I answer, smiling cheekily. "And maybe more. Why? Are you afraid I'll steal the attention away from your job?"

"No." He checks his watch. "I still have plenty of time left."

I step a little closer and lean forward. "Then why not spend some time with me?"

His brows furrow and the left side of his lip curls up for a second. "Correct me if I'm wrong but are you hitting on me?"

"Is that a crime?" I murmur, licking my lips.

His eyes are half-mast now. "That depends on what you consider a crime. You have a husband, don't you?"

"Yes, so?" I raise an eyebrow.

He cocks his head, a smile slowly building on his face. "What did you have in mind?"

I lean in and whisper in his ear, "You. Me. That room in the back of that obscure hallway."

When I arch my back and look out into the room, I can clearly spot Phillip watching me. I don't give a damn what he thinks. I'm going for it. I actually want him to see what I'm about to do.

Phoenix turns to me. His eyes are narrowed, and his tongue darts out to lick his bottom lip. Then he brings the glass to his mouth and chugs down all the remaining champagne.

No words come from his mouth. Instead, he puts down the glass and checks the room before grabbing my hand and dragging me down the hallway to that one room I mentioned. With one last glance to see if anyone's following us, he opens the door, pulls us both inside, and slams it shut before closing the lock.

"You seduced the wrong man, lady," he says.

When he steps closer, I take a step back, taunting him to come and get me. Only one step and I'm out of space to flee. This is just a small room they use to store tables and chairs for parties. I picked it exactly because it's obscure and the door can be locked from the inside. This isn't the first time I've been to a party at this venue. Nor is this my first rodeo.

"Why's that?" I ask.

"You know exactly why. It's the reason you picked me as your target in the first place. Women like you are all the same." He pushes aside a table to come near me.

"Oh? So you have experience with this? Tell me more," I retort.

"Plenty, but there's always room to add one more," he growls.

When he's in front of me, he places his hands on the table behind me and corners me. "Are you afraid?"

He leans forward, his face inches away from mine as if he's gauging how I'll react.

I shake my head.

"You should be," he whispers.

"Yes," I whimper when his lips come so close I can feel his hot breath on my skin.

"My jobs are the kind that gets people killed. You come seeking love from the devil himself," he whispers, chuckling. "Why?"

His lips are inches away from mine, and I arch to meet his mouth, but he won't let me kiss him. "I need it," I say.

"Are you that desperate?" he asks.

I frown. "Are you trying to persuade me not to do this or something?"

"I'm trying to save you your marriage," he says, frowning. "And your safety."

"I don't care," I say, closing my eyes.

"You just want me to take you," he says. "Like a needy housewife."

"Yes," I say, trying not to sound pathetic. I just threw all of my morals out of the window. Do I care?

Not even a little bit. Anything for the sake of vengeance.

"All right. I'll fuck you, missy. I'll fuck you so hard you won't be able to walk away from this party without wobbling legs."

"Fuck, yes ..." I mutter.

He smashes his lips onto mine before I can say anything else.

His lips are ruthless, overtaking my mouth like he wants to devour me whole. He isn't gentle or sweet. He just takes what he wants, kissing me full on the lips with raw excitement. His tongue swipes over my mouth, probing so I open my mouth and let him in. His neediness blows me away; his kisses demanding as he swoops me off the floor and places me on the table. I moan into his mouth as he grabs my arms and forces his mouth onto mine. I can hardly breathe.

"You wanted this, so now I'll take what I want the way I want it."

His hand moves to my dress, which he scrunches up until his hands are gripping my bare waist. From there he rips down my panties in one go, almost tugging me off the table. I barely manage to hold on.

"Holy shit," I mutter as he kicks them aside and places his hand on my neck, pulling me in for another kiss.

"Shut up and enjoy the ride, Princess."

Princess. I rarely hear that nickname. It feels good to hear it, though.

No time to react. He pulls my hair back roughly, and his lips press a kiss on my neck, sucking so hard that it leaves a mark. They drag down toward my chest until he reaches the top of my dress. With one big tug, he rips it down, exposing my breast.

I squeal. "Be careful."

His grip on my hair tightens as he pulls my head back. "No, Princess. You don't get to decide how to play this game. You came to the lion's den. Now, you do what the lion wants. And I want to fill up your tight pussy with my cum. Think you can handle that?"

I nod, swallowing. "Not without a condom, though," I add.

He cocks his head, an amused look flashing on his face. "You think I would risk my own health for some pussy, Princess? Even if your fucking pussy was made out of pure gold, I wouldn't risk it. Now, lie down," he growls.

He pushes me down before I can say anything. My head hits the table as he spreads my legs and presses his thumb right on top of my clit. "Let's get this pussy nice and wet, shall we?"

I pant and squirm from his touch, which is impossibly good. My head is spinning, my heart is racing, and my body is so goddamn ready for this man … this man who defies everything I should involve myself in.

But I want it. I need it.

Even if this man takes from me what he wants

without control, I still want what he offers. This rage feels incredible, powerful, like a drug. I can't get enough. I gave him permission to use me, and now I want the beast unleashed.

This man is my ultimate fantasy, what I've always dreamed of doing but never dared because of the meaning of the rock on my ring finger. This man … this man is danger incarnated.

He'll be the death of me.

***

Present

The memory repeats itself in my head, and I can't get rid of the shudder caused by the thought of our short affair. Arthur has put on a gloomy face, his frown seemingly permanent. Of course, he wouldn't like me telling him this. It's like holding a lollypop in front of a child and then putting it in your own mouth. Arthur wants what I had with that man. He's wanted it for years, but it wasn't right, and we both knew that.

I sigh. "I'm sorry; I shouldn't be telling you this."

"No, it's okay."

"Ma'am?" The police standing in the doorway again suddenly distract me.

"Oh, you're back," I say.

I wonder how long they've been standing there, and if they heard everything I said. Will they use it against me?

"Do you have any news?" I ask quickly.

"Well, there's been an examination of your husband's body, and what they found wasn't what we were expecting."

I slam my mouth shut, afraid of what they're going to say.

"I think you'd better sit down," they say to Arthur as he gets up from his chair.

"Tell me what happened to my brother," he says. "It wasn't just an accident, was it?"

"No."

I hold my breath.

It feels like I'm choking.

"Phillip Starr was poisoned."

My whole world falls to pieces the moment he speaks the words.

Everything I know will change forever.

I knew it the moment I saw the light leave his eyes and his lifeless arms rest on the steering wheel. The crash didn't cause his death. My husband was murdered.

"Murdered?" I mutter.

My eyes widen. The horror sinks in.

And then the real shock smacks me in the face like a brick.

I know how he died … he died because of me.

CHAPTER 5

PHOENIX

During the party …

With a drink in my hand, I watch my target vehemently. I have to time this perfectly, wait for the time to surreptitiously make my move. It's already quite suspicious that I'm just standing here at the bar, doing nothing but eyeballing the partygoers while slurping drinks. I've already had a few people glance at me with disgusted looks on their face. Each time, I look straight into their eyes until they get so creeped out they just turn their heads and leave. I love fucking with people. In the literal sense of the word as well, of course.

Especially that girl standing next to her supposed husband. Fuck, it's so wrong. She's like half his age, and all he does is grope other women. I've seen his hands all over that other woman's butt several times, even though they're presumably friends. I don't understand why she accepts it. I would have killed the son of a bitch a long time ago.

Suddenly, she turns her head toward me, and I'm awestruck at the furious look on her face. That sparkle in her eyes … I recognize it … it's the thirst for vengeance. Lucky for the both of us, the booze is over here.

I wait until she approaches me with her hips swaying back and forth in that white dress of hers. The fake smile plastered on her face pisses me off to no end because it makes me want to shake some sense into her. What the fuck is she doing here and why the fuck did she marry that man? Although, I think she might be asking herself that same question right now.

I've noticed her checking me out. It's been a long time since a woman actively wanted my attention; most of the time, they're scared for their lives. I can't say I don't enjoy it, although I could crush the glass in my hands right now. I hate it when I'm distracted from my target, but damn, this fucking girl … I just want to fuck some sense into her. Maybe I'll do just that.

She's too pretty to let go. Fucking wasn't on my to-do list tonight, but I'll gladly put her on it. I'd be a fool to turn that down. Besides, she's the wife of the man I'm going to kill. I'd call that an added bonus.

***

VANESSA

Later on at the party …

Phoenix wipes the lipstick stains from his cheek as I put my panties back on and pull my dress back together, trying to make it look like less of a mess. The content smirk on his face, coupled with my insatiable hunger for revenge, is shameful. It was worth it. I want to see the look on Phillip's face the moment he sees me walking out of this room, all flushed and high on endorphins. The only thing Phillip isn't able to give me; pleasure.

When Phoenix throws the condom in the trash, he turns to open the door.

"Hey," I say. "Am I ever going to see you again?"

"What do you mean? We're both at the same party, and I'm not leaving until I finish the job."

"I mean … after the party." I swallow, unsure of what I should say, if I should even say anything. What we did was unspeakable, loathsome, and we did it anyway. There's some sort of dark bond between us now, something invisible that I can't explain or even put into words. All I know is that we share something that no one else at this party can even fathom. Something primal, something vicious. Something evil.

"That's not up to me," he says, running his fingers through his coal black hair.

I get off the table as he holds the door open and waits for me to approach. "Then who is it up to?" I ask.

Cocking his head, he gazes at me without speaking a word. I refuse to pass him before he does, facing him with equal determination.

"You," he says.

I frown, but he doesn't allow me to ask another question. He simply leaves the room without me. I guess chivalry has its limits.

I follow him outside, glancing sideways to catch Phillip's eyes narrowing and honing in on me. The moment our eyes lock, my body explodes in pure euphoria, and a devilish smile appears on my face, my heart pumping adrenaline through my veins. I've succeeded in my goal; the ultimate payback.

I follow my one-time lover to the bar where he orders another drink.

"You still following me?" he asks.

"You say that as if you dislike it."

"That's because I still have a job to do, and you're distracting me quite a bit with your voluptuous body."

I smile at him, leaning in to place my hand on his shoulder, making sure Phillip is watching. "I'll distract you anytime."

He turns his head ever so slightly. "Taking women is like sipping wine. Only take a sip. Otherwise, they might overpower you."

I chuckle. "Touché." I lean forward to grab a drink off the table. "I'd rather be the wine than the vinegar, though."

"I enjoyed tasting you, missus," he murmurs. "But all good things must come to an end."

"No more Princess? Oh, boo."

He leans in to whisper in my ear. "Not here, no, but in my mind, you'll always be."

I grin, getting all hot again just from thinking about his hands on my hips.

I look at Phillip, who's almost crushing his glass in his hand. I love the look on his face, like someone just stomped on his balls while he was lying on the ground, begging for mercy. I chug down my drink. I don't think I would stop jumping, though.

"You should get back to your husband. I'm sure he's not too pleased to see you." He laughs a bit. When I look at him, he's holding a glass in his hands, one he wasn't holding before. "Here, take this with you." He smirks, his tongue darting out to lick the barbell underneath his lip. "To ease his pain."

I smile back. "Good thinking. You and I make a great team."

"Keep that fantasy to yourself. There's no you in this team." He points at himself. "I have some things to do. Now, go on. Go back to your husband and give him his drink."

He pushes the glass into my hand and nudges me

toward Phillip. I hesitantly walk toward him, constantly looking back at Phoenix, wondering if he'll disappear. The further I get away from him, the more the gravity of what I've done sinks in. There is something about him, something in his eyes that I shouldn't ignore. Something vicious, just like before, only this time it has nothing to do with fucking. They're the eyes of a killer.

Why did he hand me this glass? And more importantly, why did I take it?

I should go back to him, but then I realize it's too late. I'm already right behind Phillip, and he's noticed me. He stops talking to the woman next to him and focuses his attention on me.

I smile. Then I glance over my shoulder.

One look is all it takes to destroy my world.

And still I hand Phillip the glass.

I should've gone with my instinct, should've walked away, but I didn't. In this one split second, I trust the wrong thing. Or maybe it wasn't trust after all … maybe it was the insatiable need for vengeance that drove me to hand the glass to Phillip.

I knew it wasn't right.

I had it coming for me.

And yet, I did it anyway.

***

Present

I gasp, taking in the news. My husband was poisoned. I should've stopped myself when I handed that glass to him, but by the time I realized, it was already too late. There was poison in his glass. Of course, it all makes sense now. He was after my husband to begin with, and now the deal is done. My husband is dead because of me. Even if I hated him with my guts, I didn't want him to die. At least, not by my own hands.

That man is a killer, and he used me as his murder weapon.

I killed my own fucking husband.

No way am I going to get away with this.

CHAPTER 6

VANESSA

Days later

Rain pours down from above, crashing down onto our umbrellas. The sky is dark with gloom, thunder booming every so often. With clattering teeth, I hold onto my black dress so it doesn't blow over my head. What a dreadful day. Not just the weather, though. Mostly the fact that we're standing in the graveyard, watching my husband's casket lower into the ground.

Arthur holds onto me, rubbing my arm as they start shoveling up the wet earth. I just watch the ordeal and try to picture myself crying. It's the least I can do, even though it's not working. Maybe thinking about it will work.

There aren't many guests at his funeral. Half of his

friends are inside, where it's warm and comfy, waiting for the rest of us to come in as well ... the other half was happy he was dead. I'm not sure which camp I belong to.

The hospital finally lets me out of their grasp after I begged them numerous times. I was so done with that place, especially after they got all suspicious about Arthur and me. As if we're not allowed to hold hands and tell each other it'll be okay. I don't care if anyone thinks it's wrong; we both needed someone who understood what we were going through.

He lost his brother, and I lost my husband. We both think Phillip is a complete douchebag. We're both happy he's gone. Glad that we finally get to spend time with each other without him looking over our shoulders.

Even if it's wrong, it's too good to deny.

I should feel upset about Phillip's death, but all I feel is anger. Toward him, but also his killer. Why was I involved? Was it an accident? Maybe my husband was supposed to die from the poison, and we weren't supposed to get into the car. Maybe it didn't go as planned, and maybe I was a loose end in the entire scheme.

If so, I bet he isn't counting on me remembering everything.

He probably knows I survived, so he must be watching us closely. I doubt he'll take the news well if he finds out I can recall the name of my husband's killer.

Waiting for the sand to fill the grave is not a good time to be pondering these things, but still I can't stop thinking about it. I never expected it to be him—the man I slept with at the party, out of all people. It's as if the devil himself played me.

Maybe he knew all along. Maybe he didn't care. Maybe I was just another conquest, just another person he could kill.

Grinding my teeth, I grab Arthur's hand and entwine my fingers with his. The glass that I gave to him poisoned my husband, but I will not go down for this. I'm not the murderer here. I will find the real one, and I will bring him to justice. Whatever the cost.

***

PHOENIX

From a distance, I watch the crowd as they bend over his grave. The umbrella I'm carrying barely keeps the rain from soaking my coat, but at least it's something. I fucking hate the rain. I prefer sunny days over any other, especially when there's a funeral. Nothing dampens a happy day more than rain, and this should be one fucking marvelous day.

I eliminated my target. The grave has been dug. The

casket containing his body has been lowered into the ground. It's truly done. Mission accomplished.

However, that woman and my stupid conscience interfering with the job really put a damper on everything. Just by rescuing her, I put myself at risk. If she remembers anything about that day, then she knows I'm the one who murdered her husband. Judging from the way she acted around me, I don't think she'd be afraid to fight me on who's responsible for his death. Even though she was the one who ultimately pulled the trigger on him, I was the one who handed her the weapon.

I don't think she'll be pleased.

The thought alone makes me grin.

I love it when people are angry with me. Makes for a good show.

She doesn't know I'm here, and she doesn't need to know. I've been watching her for days, listening to conversations, hoping to catch something that indicates she remembers. If she's going to tell anyone what she knows, I'd rather be prepared than sorry.

The way she holds the hand of the man next to her pisses me off, though. Not just because I fucked her, hell no, I'm never jealous. No, I hate it because it means they're getting close … and whoever she gets close to will learn the truth eventually. No one is safe. No one can be trusted. Everyone will turn into my enemy in the blink of an eye.

I'd rather not cause more deaths than necessary,

but if she starts hunting for the truth, I can't promise anything. Not even if she begs me to … although, of course, I would love to hear it. I can already hear her raspy voice as she asks me to spare her life, touching my body with those soft hands of hers. So desperate to save herself, that she'd even let me fuck her … over and over again until finally I'd kill her anyway. Because that's just how I roll.

I have one rule for anyone who dares to come into my life; don't fuck with me, or I'll fucking kill you. I make zero exceptions. Just because you have a vagina doesn't mean you're any less likely to die.

I snort as the crowd near the grave starts to walk away, with the exception of Mister and Missus hold-hands. She leans up against him, and he wraps his hands tightly around her body. Aww … they're hugging. How sweet. *Barf.*

If I wasn't fucking forced to watch her and make sure she didn't tell on me, I would've gone over there and thrown him into the grave with that other bastard. They both belong there anyway. Yeah, I know they're brothers, but I also know neither of them is good, even though this one portrays himself to be. Fucking liars, all of them, including her. They're all living a lie, and they know it. And I'm here wondering when the fuck they're all going to wake up and see what they're doing.

Too bad for me, it's only going to get worse. The guy next to her caresses her cheek as she gazes into his eyes. She looks upset, confused even, but I can't tell well from this distance. However, what I *can* clearly see is when he leans in to kiss her.

Fucking hell.

Now I want to kill him, too.

Luckily, she takes her lips off his very quickly, and she leans away from him. I guess dear brother-in-law didn't quite cut it. Of course … no kiss matches up to mine. I'm probably still haunting her dreams … and nightmares … and I wouldn't have it any other way.

CHAPTER 7

VANESSA

When Arthur presses his lips onto mine, it feels like I've gone to heaven. A piece of me floats away as I let him kiss me, dazed by his sudden affection. It makes me feel wanted, something I've not experienced in a long time.

However, it isn't right. Not now. Not here. Even though kissing him is the best feeling in the world right now … I can't kiss Arthur. Not yet. It's too soon. It feels wrong. What would people think? Phillip's death is still too fresh.

I place my hand on Arthur's chest and push back, allowing room between us. "I can't," I murmur.

"I'm sorry. I shouldn't have," he says, looking down at the ground. "I just hate to see you unhappy like this."

My hand instinctively reaches for his face to caress his cheek. "I know. It's okay."

He frowns. "I'm trying to fight it, Vanessa. I really am." He sighs. "This is all my fault."

"Stop, don't say that. You aren't the cause of his death."

"No, but I'm making things more confusing than they already are."

"How?" I ask, cocking my head.

He smiles at me. "I've always desired you, Vanessa. I won't lie. I tried to hide it for your sake … for my brother's sake."

I place my finger on his lips. "Say no more."

He nods, realizing now is not the time for love.

Now is the time for mourning. Even if we don't feel bad about his death, the very least we can do is respect those who do.

I turn my head away to catch a fresh breeze when I notice a man standing between two graves not far from here. I can't see much, except his dark suit and umbrella, and the way his shades glisten in the light of the lamp as he turns around.

He was watching us.

Taking a deep breath, I say, "Arthur, I have to go."

"Why? Where are you going?" he asks.

"I … I just want to be alone for a while. I hope you don't mind. You go sit with the rest of the people, okay?" I turn around and start walking toward the man who's walking away at an increasing speed.

"Okay …" Arthur says, but I'm no longer listening.

All I can focus on is that man with the umbrella as he walks toward the exit of the premises. He wasn't just standing there; he was spying on us, and I want to know why. Because if my instincts are right, I know who he is.

What I'm doing is dangerous, and I'm fully aware of the consequences of my actions. I could be hurt or, worse, killed. However, I need answers. I have to know *why*.

The faster he walks, the more I speed up, which quickly turns into running. When he heads around the corner, I lose sight of him, but I know he's going to the parking lot. He must be. I mean, there's nowhere else to go.

Except as I pass the gate, I don't see anyone.

With my hand above my eyes to block the rain, I gaze around. The parking lot is completely empty and there's not a soul in sight.

I make my way toward my car, constantly looking around me because I'm afraid the guy might jump me. I wonder if he already raced off with his car, but that wouldn't make any sense because then I would have heard something. He must be hiding somewhere, in which case it only makes it scarier. I have to get somewhere safe, quickly.

When I get to my car, I turn off the locks which beep and then jerk open the door, so I can get inside fast and slam the door shut before anyone tries to come in. My breathing is rapid and my heart beats out of control as I stare through the front window, looking for him. Rain clatters on the window, almost making it impossible to see anything, so I turn on the windshield wipers. Shivering, I turn on the heater and try to calm myself down. Maybe it wasn't him at all. Maybe I'm just being paranoid.

"Hello, Vanessa."

I scream, but a gloved hand smothering my face muffles my sounds. "Be quiet."

Squealing, I try to pull his fingers away from my mouth, but he comes around from the other side and points something sharp at my throat. "I said be quiet!"

Air enters my nose with short, shallow breaths as I suppress the tears. It's him. I was right. He was watching us.

"Don't try anything. Don't even fucking move a muscle," he says gruffly.

I nod my head, but stop immediately when I feel the sharp edge of the blade against my flesh.

"Feel this?" he asks, as he pushes the blade further. It's so sharp; I can feel it cut me just a bit. Enough for a droplet of blood to roll down and fall into my lap. "It's very sharp and it just loves some fresh blood, especially when it comes from a pretty girl like you."

I swallow when he says that, fear settling in my veins.

"You try *anything*, and I will kill you. Do you

understand?" he growls.

I nod, blinking away the impending tears.

"Good. I'll take my hand away but not this knife. You'd better stick to what you just agreed to, or it's going to cut straight through your neck."

When he slides his glove off my face, I suck a big breath. Then the questions come rolling out. "You killed him. Are you going to kill me too now?"

"No." He laughs, running his fingers through his coal black hair. I don't dare look back at his face, but I can see his eyes narrow at me through the rearview mirror. "I might be a murderer, but I don't just kill anyone, unless they get in my way."

"You poisoned my husband!"

His lip quirks up into a smile. "Well, technically, you did."

I frown. "You won't get away with this."

He cocks his head. "The question you should be asking is: Will you?"

"How dare you? You want to put the blame on me, but I'm not the murderer here."

He leans in, so close that my breath hitches when he whispers into my ear, "Oh, yes you are ..." He taps the knife against my throat like it's a toy. "Stop lying to yourself, Vanessa. You and I both know you're full of it. But you can't fool me."

He slips back into his seat, watching me while tapping his fingers on his leg. My lips part, but I don't know how to respond. I don't know what to say that will get him to talk without cutting my head off.

"You ruined everything ..." I say after a while.

"Oh, really? Why is that? Because I killed your traitorous, adulterous husband?" With his teeth, he tugs on the barbell underneath his lip, as if he's enjoying this.

"Screw you," I spit, but when he pushes the knife into my skin, I lean into my seat again. "I won't go down for this."

"Neither will I, sweet cheeks," he mocks. "But one of us has to. I'm betting it's going to be you. It's not looking good as it is, especially not with everyone seeing you run off with some other guy at the party."

My lungs suddenly feel constricted. I can't breathe.

"Imagine the tabloids. Scorned wife kills unfaithful husband out of revenge. I can already see the headlines in front of me."

He makes a frame with his free hand and then makes a snapping sound in my direction. I blink a couple of times, expecting the knife to bury itself deep in my throat. I don't know why he wouldn't do it. I'm the only one who knows the truth. If I'm dead, the secret is buried with me. If I were him, I would kill me right now. Not that I don't want to live. I'm just stating the facts.

"Don't you think it's ironic? Perfect, really. Like the opposite of a fucking fairy tale." He laughs out loud, making all the hairs on the back of my neck stand up.

"What do you want from me?" I ask. "Are you just

here to laugh in my face after killing my husband?"

Within the blink of an eye, his face turns all serious again. "I'm here to tell you to give up now. Don't look for me. Don't follow me. Don't try to find me. Don't for a second think that you can pin this on me."

He pushes the knife further into my throat, causing another tiny stream of blood to roll down my neck. "Make no mistake. I *will* kill you, and it won't be as gentle as the way your husband died."

Immediately, I'm reminded of the car crash but, of course, he's referring to the poison. Phillip was never meant to get into his car, and yet, he did it anyway.

"This is just a warning, but I will come back for you if you try anything. You understand?" he says with a low voice that causes goosebumps to scatter across my skin.

I nod quickly. "Yes." The moment the word spills from my mouth, I already know it's a lie … and I think he knows, too.

He leans closer, breathing hot air onto my skin, which tingles in an oh so wrong way. "Good girl. See you around, Princess."

And then the knife suddenly disappears along with him.

Holding my neck to prevent more blood from spilling, I turn around in my seat, but by that time, the door has already slammed shut. With his umbrella above his head, he strolls to his own car not far from mine. As he opens the door and sits down, he keeps his eyes focused on my car. Our eyes connect, and for a moment, I'm awestruck. He didn't kill me. Instead, he walked away with only a threat … One I don't believe, but a threat nonetheless.

As he drives backward, I can clearly see his license plate. It surprises me that he didn't rip it off prior to our meeting. He probably wants me to see it and remember it, forcing me to choose. Act on it, or leave it alone and forget about it all.

He's tempting me … persuading me to act. Well, I will take on this dare. May the best liar win.

CHAPTER 8

VANESSA

The next day

For days, I feel followed. Wherever I go, someone's always behind me. Whether it's a car, a person stalking closely, or suspicious coincidences, everything makes me feel nervous. It's as if I'm losing my mind. Half of it probably is my imagination and the other part … well, let's just say that a car with a very peculiar license plate has been showing up on my street every so often. It's like he's spying on me, waiting for me to take the bait, but I know I won't catch him. Not before he catches me.

The only thing I can do is go after him in a way he least expects it. Visit him in a place he wouldn't think I'd go. He probably thinks I don't have the guts for it, but I'll prove him wrong. I will find the evidence I need and show the police who the real killer is. That way they won't be able to pin it on me.

Sliding aside the curtains, I look out the window and stare at the license plate. The numbers are etched into my memory; I've seen them so many times. I guess it shouldn't be too hard for my friends at the police station to find out who it belongs to.

I make a quick call to my father. "Father."

"Hi, honey. How are you? We haven't spoken since … well, are you feeling better?"

He wasn't even at the funeral. He was too busy using a pair of scissors to cut a ribbon around a new opera building that just opened in town. Guess some things are more important than others are. Oh well, I can't blame him. I would've given anything to be anywhere but at that grave.

"Yeah, much better," I lie. I'm being threatened not to spill the truth to the police while they're about to find out it was me who gave the glass containing the poison to Phillip. I'd hardly call that 'better.'

"Hey, I was wondering … Could you get a license plate number checked for me?" I ask with a sweet voice.

"Honey … We talked about this."

"I know, Father, but this is important. I promise you, you'll want to help me on this."

"I can't just abuse my connections."

"Please?" I ask with an even sweeter voice.

He sighs. "Oh, all right."

"Thank you!" I say. "I'll send you the number via text."

"Don't thank me yet. I don't know if they will tell me what you want to know, but I can try."

"Oh, I'm sure you'll get it done. They always listen to you. You're such an inspiration for the city!" I really need to stop, before I barf in my mouth.

"I'll do my best."

"Thank you. Let me know when you get it."

"Should be within a couple of days."

"Okay. Loved talking to you. Bye." I hang up the phone before he can say anything else. It's not unusual to get what I want without being very nice. This is just how things go in our family. We use and abuse to our heart's content.

Oh well, time for my treatment at the spa. I have to do something while I wait for the call anyway … besides, it's not like I'm followed or anything, and that I have to keep up the charade. Oh, but wait, I do.

Which is why I pretend that I'm not doing anything out of the ordinary, as usual. I'm good at playing the dumbass. It provides a good cover so I can surprise people when I waltz all over them. They never see what's coming their way until it's too late.

I need the info my father will supply, so there's plenty of time to waste.

All good things come to those who wait.

***

One hour later…

When I'm back home, the first thing I do is lounge on the couch with a cold drink. I'm finally able to have a living room to myself without Phillip claiming the television. You know, I never knew how wonderful it would be *not* to have him around. You know what? I'm glad he died. I'm not going to lie. I hated his guts, and there's no point in denying it. I almost feel bad for wanting him gone even sooner. Almost.

Taking a deep breath, I look out the window and enjoy the short bursts of sunlight when all of the sudden the doorbell rings.

Pablo, our housekeeper, goes to open it. "Mrs. Starr. It's the police."

Frowning, I get up from my seat. "What do they want?"

"Could you come to the door, please, Mrs. Starr," I hear the police call out.

I tiptoe to the door in my ballet shoes, only to find a man staring at me with parted lips and a cold look on his face.

"What's the matter?" I ask. "Found anything new in my husband's case?"

"Yes, ma'am. As a matter of fact, we found out what poisoned him." My heart sinks into my shoes. "We have to take you to the station."

"What?" I say, my breath hitching in my throat.

"I'm sorry, but we have to take you in for questioning."

Before I can say anything, the police officer has already stepped into my house and grabbed my hand. "I'll escort you to the car."

I nod slowly, but my body is going numb. As if I'm in a trance from which I can't wake up.

"I'll watch the house for you, Mrs. Starr," Pablo says.

"Yes …" I murmur, as the officers escort me to the car.

I've never sat in a police car. This will be my first time.

And as a criminal, too.

This is all his fault, fucking Phoenix Sullivan. He's trying to pin it on me, but I won't let him get away with it. One way or another, I'll get out of this mess, and when I do, he'll burn for this.

***

Two hours later…

"I already told you that I'm innocent."

"Yes, ma'am, you keep saying that, but all evidence points in your direction."

I sigh out loud. "Yes, I gave that glass to him, but I didn't know it was filled with poison."

"It's a little too much of a coincidence."

"What is?" I frown.

"Well, considering your husband's … affairs and the current state of your marriage, it's not looking good from our perspective."

"You base your conclusions on the tabloids," I say, leaning forward. "Shame on you. You should know better than that."

"Not entirely, Mrs. Starr. Our sources place your husband at a local strip club and multiple other venues where there are walkers on the streets."

"You mean hookers. Call it for what it is." I make a face. I'm seriously not impressed with their efforts.

"We understand your frustration, but we have substantial evidence against you."

"No, you don't. All you have is some glass, which I supposedly gave him, and my supposed anger toward my husband for cheating. That's not evidence, that's circumstantial, at best. You're just trying to pin it on me, just like the real killer."

"And who do you suppose this real killer is then?" they ask, as if they don't know it's not me.

"Phoenix Sullivan. And he's still out there on the streets right now, doing his business. He's probably off killing someone else as we speak."

The police officer smiles at me. I know he doesn't believe me, but they can't keep me here forever, either.

"So, is this conversation finished? Can I go home now?" I ask.

"We still have a few questions …"

"You don't have anything against me, so you're holding me against my will. If I'm not under arrest, I'm free to go. So let me out." I look him in the eyes. "Now."

He sighs. "All right. If you're not willing to help us."

"I am, but you're not listening."

He grabs a pen and a notebook. "Tell us where he lives then. I will go and talk to him."

"Like talking will help," I say. "He won't tell you the truth, if that's what you're thinking." I laugh. "Imagine that, a killer telling you that he murdered someone." Now I can't stop laughing.

He clears his throat to interrupt me. "We will check it out. For now, you're free to go. But that doesn't mean you're not still a suspect."

"I know. Don't worry, I won't run," I say as I get up from my seat. "You think I'm a criminal, but you're wrong, and I will prove it."

"Please don't do anything against the law," he says, also getting up as I walk to the door.

I smile as I pass him, pausing for a second. "I'll see you soon then."

Sooner than he thinks.

CHAPTER 9

VANESSA

That night

When I get home, I'm exhausted, and the rain pouring down on my head isn't helping either. I feel miserable after today, totally defeated from the news that I'm really a suspect in my husband's murder. Now, more than ever, I feel the loneliness creeping up inside me, and it makes me want to scream.

But I don't. Instead, I cling onto my phone and call Arthur's number.

"Hey," I say when he picks up. "It's me."

"Vanessa. Are you all right? You sound sick."

I sigh. "No, actually, not at all."

"What happened?"

I sniff. "They questioned me. They think I killed

Phillip."

"Oh, no ..." I can hear him take a deep breath. "That's not good news at all, especially not after ... well, you know."

"I know; it's just a little too much right now."

"Are you all by yourself?" he asks.

"Yes, but ..."

"Come to my house then. We can talk about it." There's not an ounce of doubt in his voice, which makes me feel like he really does care about me.

"Okay ..."

"Just come over," he says.

I swallow. "I'll have to think about it."

"Don't think for too long," he says, chuckling.

"Thank you for... Well, you know," I say, clearing my throat. "Bye."

I end the call before he can say anything else. I know what he wants. By inviting me to his home, he doesn't just want to talk. I know him too well for that. He's always been there for me the moment I need it the most. He gives me what I need—love, which is exactly what I crave right now.

I feel so bad for wanting it, but my entire body is shaking with need. Today has been such a bad day, and nothing will make it better except to be with the only person who cares about me. Urges overwhelm me, so I do what any sane person would do. I turn around and go back to my car, switching my brain off. I don't think about what I'm going to do, I just act on my feelings.

After all, everyone needs to feel loved.

***

Thirty minutes later …

As I stand in front of Arthur's door, I bite my lip, contemplating on whether or not to ring the bell. The guilt has wormed its way back into my heart, telling me it isn't right, that I shouldn't even be considering this, but what else am I supposed to do? I can't keep wallowing in self-pity. I can't stay alone forever. And just because he is Phillip's brother doesn't make it bad … Phillip isn't here anymore, there is no more connection. Nothing separates Arthur and me. Nothing stands in our way.

The decision is made for me as the door opens anyway. Arthur's standing in the doorway with a half undone shirt, and from what I can tell by peeking, he's packing quite a few muscles. For his age, he looks damn fine. I guess he does like to work out once in a while.

"Vanessa, you're here," he says, frowning.

"Surprised?" I say, patting my hair, which is soaked.

"Yeah, a little. Come in, come in," he says, ushering me inside.

I walk inside, and he closes the door behind us. His house looks quite cozy, not big like mine, but comfortable. The lights have a nice red glow to them, and the temperature inside the house is just right. Warm enough for me to stop shivering and finally dry my hair.

Arthur walks to the kitchen. "You must be cold. Let me make some tea."

"Oh, that would be great," I say. "It's such bad weather outside."

"I'm surprised you came through this storm," he says, chuckling. "I wasn't expecting it, but it's a nice surprise."

"Hmm … Well, I did question if I should for a second."

"I could've come to your house too, but I didn't want to overstep. I mean, it's still fresh and everything." He comes back with tea as I sit down on the couch. "I wasn't sure if it was appropriate."

"Oh, I get you," I say. "It's okay. Thanks."

He puts down the tea and sits down beside me. I grab my cup and take a sip, which instantly warms up my body.

"Are you cold? I can grab a blanket," he says, unsure whether I'll allow him to sit next to me or not.

"No, I'm fine," I say, smiling.

There's an uncomfortable vibe between us that I just can't seem to shake. Every time I look at him, he gazes back with this comforting smile that makes me shiver. I want to say something, but I have no clue what and I guess he doesn't either, looking at his parted lips. We laugh a little and I take another sip of my tea to break the weird mood.

"So … What did the police ask you?" Arthur says.

I swallow away the lump in my throat. "They accused me of killing him."

He frowns. "Why?"

"Because he was poisoned." I look at him, my eyes getting watery again. "They think I gave it to him on purpose."

"Oh, no …" he says, putting his hand in front of his mouth. "So you're the prime suspect now?"

"I didn't do it, Arthur." I put down my cup. "Yes, I gave him the glass, but I didn't know it had poison in it. They don't believe me." My voice is getting higher with every passing second, and I feel like I'm going to break. "They think I did it on purpose. Please, you have to believe me, Arthur. I'm not a murderer."

"Shhh …" He puts his arms around me and hugs me tight. "I believe you."

His hands are on my back, caressing me while I listen to his deep breaths. It calms me down to be in his vicinity. I just hope he believes me. I don't want to lose anyone else.

"Are you sure?" I ask. "I mean, they could come and question you, too."

He grabs my arms and pushes me back. "I believe only you, Vanessa. Always. I trust you." His hand drifts to my cheek, his thumb stroking me tenderly. "How could I not believe you? I feel too much for you to ever be able to ignore your words."

My lips quiver as he leans forward and looks me in the eye. "I don't know what to say … I feel …" I shudder, sucking a breath. "I don't know what I should feel."

"Me neither, but I know it feels good." He grabs my hand and places it on his chest. "I feel it in here, and always when I'm around you. I know you feel it, too. I can't ignore it anymore."

"But I'm a married woman," I say, leaning into his soft hand cupping my face, which feels so nice.

"*Were.* And my brother wasn't good to you. He didn't deserve your love." His hand moves to my chin to lift my head. "Let me comfort you."

He leans in further, and I let him. Before I realize it, his lips are on mine, kissing me softly. It feels so good … so normal … like it was always supposed to be this way. Arthur has always admired me, loved me, even from a distance, when he couldn't come near me. But with his brother no longer here, we finally have the chance to try something new.

His kisses are gentle and soothing, so good that I want more. I wrap my arms around his neck and invite him even closer. Our kiss becomes deeper the more seconds pass. I can't get enough. It feels like all the floodgates have opened and all that I've been holding inside comes pouring out.

His tongue dips out to probe the rim of my mouth and seduce me into giving in and opening up completely. I do what my gut tells me, turning my brain off, enjoying the moment. Desperate to get closer, I press my body to his. He slowly crawls on top of me, pushing me into the sofa with my back as he rests on top of me. His kisses become faster and his hands start roaming across my body. I squirm underneath him as he cups my ass and squeezes, a groan audible through all the kissing. I love the way it sounds, the rawness of his need, and wonder how long he has kept this hunger stored inside him.

His hands find their way to the hem of my dress and slowly creep up underneath, dragging the fabric with them. A moan rolls over my lips as his hands slide up toward my breasts, and he covers my mouth with his. I can feel his hard-on poking me through his pants, and I immediately feel the urge to push his zipper down and take him right here, right now. I don't care about the consequences of what we're doing. I don't care about anything, and that's okay. We both need love, and we found it in each other.

"I want you so badly," he whispers as he drags his lips to my ear.

"Me, too," I say. "I want you, too." My body arches to meet his as he cups my breast and massages it, giving ample attention to my nipple with his thumb.

"Is it wrong?" he groans, pressing a kiss to my neck.

"No …" I moan as he rubs his cock against me.

"God, I feel so bad," he says, hissing while biting his lip. "I just can't stop myself."

"Don't stop," I whisper. "I need it. I need you." He looks me in the eye as I say, "Let's be bad together."

***

PHOENIX

"How long are we going to be here?" my girlfriend asks, tugging on my arm.

I jerk my arm and take my eyes off the binoculars. "As long as I want to."

"Why? You said you'd take me out," she says.

I frown. "Yes, and we're outside. Your point?"

She rolls her eyes. "You know that's not what I meant."

"I don't care. I have more important things on my mind right now."

She makes a face. "Oh, c'mon. What's so fun about spying on a girl anyway when you got me?" She flaunts her body by pushing her tits in my face.

I shove her back in her seat. "Sit down. I don't have time for you now."

She sighs out loud. "Fine." She folds her arms and gazes outside the other window. Finally, she's off my case. God, that woman can be annoying sometimes. Like now, I wonder why the fuck I ever agreed to live together … but then I remember it's because she's such a good sucker. She's always ready, willing, and I can take what I want when I want. And I love me a good fuck every day. Why not take it from her if she offers it so willingly?

Besides, it's not like she's useful for anything else. She gets on my nerves a lot, especially when I'm trying to do something like now.

I return my attention to the view I had through the binoculars and look through the window. I can clearly see Vanessa talking with some dude who I presume is Phillip's brother. I'm curious to see if she's going to tell him anything about me. I've been keeping an eye on her the entire time, just to see if she would make a move. I assume she's waiting for the right time or the right person ... someone like his brother would make sense. Plus, she *is* the type of girl who would try and get the police on my tracks. It's not a question of *if*, but when.

My grip on the binoculars tightens as I spot him inching closer to her and touching her face. A jolt of anger rushes through me, something I'm not familiar with, as I rarely get jealous. But damn, the moment he puts his lips on hers, a raging fire boils inside me, bursting out through my mouth. I growl, almost breaking the binoculars in my hands. How dare he fucking touch her? She's mine. I fucked her first. I don't fucking care what happens next. I just want her to think about me, and only me.

In a fit of rage, I throw the binoculars at the

window, almost breaking the glass.

"Hey! Be careful," my girlfriend says.

"Fuck off ..." I mutter, rubbing my forehead. Why can't I stop thinking about her? She means nothing to me. And yet, I can't stop wondering if she'll expose me as the killer, *and* as someone she fucked. I should be the only one on her mind right now, but I'm not, and it's pissing me off.

"No, what the hell is wrong with you?" my girlfriend yells.

"Shut up," I say, narrowing my eyes at her. "I don't want to hear your yammering."

She frowns, pursing her lips. "Well, you're in a great mood. I knew I shouldn't have left the house with you. It was a mistake to even think you'd finally go out with me like normal couples do."

"I said shut the fuck up!" I scream at her face, which makes her back away.

She swallows, and I lean back in my chair, grabbing the steering wheel like it's my lifeline. "Don't talk to me right now."

"Sorry," she says softly.

Blowing out a big breath, I turn on the engine and drive away.

I don't want to see, hear, or even think of anything that involves Vanessa Starr anymore. I can't take that woman consuming my mind. I have to burn the image out of my memories quickly, and there's only one way I know how to make that happen.

Either she does what I want, which is not talking to *anyone*, or heads are going to roll.

***

VANESSA

Arthur smiles and then kisses me again, and I hungrily kiss him back while undoing the button of his jeans. They slide down as I cup his ass and bring him closer to me. His hands slip down between my legs to cup my pussy and circle around my clit. I breathe heavily into his mouth, warmth flowing through my body as he starts toying with my most sensitive spot. All I can think about is having him inside me, so I pull down his boxer shorts, letting his cock spring out.

"Are you sure?" he murmurs, kissing my lips while still playing with my pussy.

"Yes, I want you," I moan. "Please …"

I'm pathetic, begging him to fuck me, but the urge is consuming me. I need him to love me. I need love … I've been deprived of it for so long, and Arthur hands it to me on a silver platter. How can I not give in?

From under his lashes, he looks at me and then hooks his fingers underneath my panties and pulls them down slowly, kissing me sensually on my collarbone. I lean up as he grabs a condom from his pants and rips it open. His cock is nicely shaped, thick but not too large, and I love the way it bounces when he sees me looking. I push the zipper on the back of my dress as far as I can and let it slide off my shoulders, just past my breasts. When my nipples peek out, the left side of his lip perks up. He rolls the condom over his dick and then lowers himself on top of me, covering my nipple with his mouth.

I moan out loud as he gives me what I need, and in return, I let him have me for the night. I don't know if this is one of many nights to come, but there's no need to worry about that now. Not when I'm delirious from his kisses.

When his hard-on pokes my entrance, I gasp, and when he thrusts, I feel complete.

"God, you feel so good," he mutters, as he slides back out and in again.

"Yes," I moan. "Fuck me, Arthur."

"Fuck?" he says, stopping his kisses for a second. "I don't want to fuck you, Vanessa. I want to love you."

I frown. "It's the same thing."

"Not in my book." He smiles, sliding aside a strand of hair from my face. He presses a kiss on my nose. "I want to love you for everything you are and give you what you need."

"What I need now is you, inside me," I whisper. "Please, do it. I don't want to think anymore. I want to feel you."

He groans as his cock pulsates, and then he thrusts again. "All right." He presses his lips to my mouth and consumes me with a deep kiss. "I love you, Vanessa. Not just today. I always have."

"I know, Arthur … I know."

"Let me love you, let me in," he murmurs as I feel the tension rise.

"Yes." The thrusts come faster and faster, and I'm reaching my climax soon.

"Give everything to me," he says.

"I'm going to come," I moan, grabbing him tight.

We exchange hot breaths, moans, and whispers as we're both about to burst. I look him in the eyes, knowing what we're doing and enjoying every single second of it. The way he gazes at me, completely enraptured, so intense that it makes me fall apart right underneath him. My body rocks with the rhythm of his thrusts as I come apart at the seams, convulsing, disappearing into bliss. And then he explodes, and I feel his warmth filling me up. A few more thrusts and he sinks down on top of me, hugging me, panting heavily. I wrap my arms around him and close my eyes … For the first time in a long time, I feel loved again.

CHAPTER 10

VANESSA

The next day, sunset

Spending the night with Arthur was just what I needed. Recuperating much-needed energy, my body felt renewed and ready for the counterattack. Phoenix may have set me up to make the police believe that I killed my husband on purpose, but that doesn't mean I'm not able to do the same to him.

I hold my pink dress hat tight as the wind almost whisks it away. I'm sitting at a table outside a bar, right across the street. With a steaming cup of tea, and the sun shining brightly against my sunglasses, I watch the scene in front of me unfold.

Phoenix steps out of his apartment building with a horrid look on his face, and he marches toward his car.

I check my watch, which signifies it's been thirty minutes since he arrived. Took him long enough.

My father texted me the address last night, so when I came home this morning, the first thing I did was pay Phoenix a visit. Too bad he wasn't there. Luckily, he's here now. Just in time for the show to start.

I wait and drink my tea until he comes back with his car, parks it in front of the door, and goes back inside. I wonder what he's doing, but I don't have to wait long for an answer. Within a few minutes, he's back, this time with a tent bag that is way too large to actually contain a tent … and much heavier too, it seems.

I guess he really doesn't give a shit who sees him. In broad daylight, he throws the bag into the backseat of his car and jumps behind the wheel.

Taking a last sip, I put down a few bills and leave my seat. Before I get into my car, I walk into an obscure alley away from the crowd and grab my phone. Swallowing and sighing, I try to make myself out of breath before I dial the numbers.

"Hello, is this the police?" I ask, trying to make my voice sound erratic.

"Yes, do you want to report a crime?"

"He's trying to kill me!" I yell.

"Who is? Where are you, ma'am?"

"Route fifty-five. Please, come quickly!"

"The cars are on their way, ma'am, hold on."

"Hurry up," I scream between, "Help!"

"Ma'am, stay on the phone, please. We're coming to your location as fast as possible."

"I can't! He just killed this other girl, and now he's coming after me."

"Ma'am, please do *not* hang up the phone."

"I can't ..." I make gurgling sounds, choking myself while doing so. Then I turn off the phone and walk away. Putting on my sunglasses, I jump into my car and drive after Phoenix.

I don't need to see his car to know where he's going.

It's where he always goes.

***

PHOENIX

I can't believe I have to fucking do this again. Burying a corpse isn't one of my favorite things to do, especially not when it's my fucking girlfriend. But there's nothing else to do about it. She's dead anyway, and I can't leave her in my apartment. The stench would make people call the police, and I can't have them on my back right now. Still, it's sad that she had to die this way. I didn't mean for it to happen, but I guess there are always unforeseen casualties in this business.

I park my car near the edge of the road and jump out, so I can open the back door and pull out the bag with her corpse in it. It's quite a strain on the muscles as I pull her out and drag her toward the sand far from the road. It's taking all my strength to get as far away as possible, but once my energy is spent, I drop the bag and take a few moments to breathe.

Right then, I hear another engine roaring behind me.

I look up and to my side and see a car parked right behind mine.

Well, fuck me.

Visitors? I guess someone's having a bad day, and it isn't me. Oh well, one more kill isn't going to make a difference.

I walk back to the car, leaving the body behind because she's dead anyway and there's no one out here to steal her body. I'm far more interested in the person who came to snoop in on my business. I wonder if there is a certain death wish floating around, or if I have an admiring fan. That would be a fun surprise.

Instead, I get a grumpy Vanessa Starr stepping out of her car with her shades tucked into the rim of her dress. Fucking hell, if it weren't for the fact that she looks like a walking fuck-doll, I would grab my gun and shoot her for even daring to come here. But I'd much rather enjoy her figure for a while; might as well while she's here anyway. And I know she wants it.

"You again," I say. "How did you find me?"

With a smug smile, she says, "Easy. This is where we always bury our secrets."

Goddammit. She's really getting on my nerves now, bringing that up. "Didn't you hear me when I told you to fuck off?" I growl.

"Oh, I did, but then again I've never been much of a good listener anyway," she says, wearing that fake smile like she always does.

I want to fuck that pretty little smile off her face.

Narrowing my eyes, I walk toward her as she leans against her car. "What the fuck are you doing here?"

"Following you," she says.

With furrowed brows, I say, "Playing with the devil will get you killed, Princess."

I place my hand on the car as she puts her back against it. "I'm not here to play games, *Phoenix*."

"Aw, really? Shame, because I was really starting to get into this game of catch." She tries to push me away, but I don't back off that easily. "Wow, settle down, girl, you don't want to enrage the beast."

"I think I already have, so I don't care anymore," she says, and then she slaps me in the face. "That's for killing my husband."

I cock my head. "You had to go and do that." I grind my teeth. "You fucking bitch."

She spits in my face, so I grab her hands and pin them to the door. "Make one more move and I'll fuck you up, right here, right now."

"Let's go, baby," she taunts.

I breathe through my nose, attempting to calm myself because I'd rather not kill a beauty like her, but damn … she's really getting on my nerves now, especially after what she's done.

"Wanna fuck me, boy?" she says.

"Been there, done that," I say, smiling at her. "I wasn't too impressed."

The look on her face goes from seductive to rage within the snap of a finger. "Fuck you!"

She kicks me in the balls. God-fucking-dammit. That fucking hurts.

She runs past me, so after catching a quick breath, I go after her. It doesn't take long for me to catch up. I jump on her back, causing her to fall into the sand and roll around.

"Get off me!" she yells.

"That's the first time I've ever heard you beg me to *not* be on top."

She tries to slap me again, but I grab her wrists and pin them down. "Not again."

"Yes, again. Think I'm going to stop? After what you did?"

"Yeah, I thought my knife on your throat was a good warning. Apparently not. Jesus Christ, all you girls are the same."

"Are what?" she says.

"Pitiful …" I spit.

"Why did you kill him?"

My nose starts to twitch, feeling the urge to kill.

"Oh, there are plenty of reasons why I killed that son of a bitch, and now I have plenty of reasons to kill you, too."

"You fucking murderer!" she yells.

"Oh, that's precious, coming from a girl like you," I say, making a face. "Pretentious, fake little princess. Jesus fucking Christ, you really have outdone yourself this time."

"Shut up, you don't know what you're talking about."

"Except, I do, or did you forget everything?"

She's quiet for a moment, taking a deep breath. "As if I'm the only fake one here. Phoenix Sullivan? Is that the name you go by now?"

"So, you *do* remember." I eye her from top to bottom, getting closer as I smell her intoxicating scent.

"I don't *want* to remember."

Frowning, I stare at her, anger seeping into my pores until I no longer feel anything but hatred for her. Again, she's proven just how much of a bitch she can be. Just by uttering those words, she's torn open a long ago closed wound that I've been trying to cover up for years.

"You bitch," I mutter. My hands immediately go for her throat.

I want her gone. I want her dead. I don't want to think about her anymore. Screw her, screw everything. She has to die. She has to be gone from this world. She has to pay for what she did … everything she and her husband did. It's all I can think about. Kill … kill … kill!

My fingers wrap so tightly around her neck that I can hear her choke on her own breath. Her fingers pry at mine in a desperate attempt to free her from my grasp, but I hold on mercilessly.

It's not until the sirens in the distance come that I realize what I'm doing. By the time the police come near, my hands are pulled from her throat, and I hear her raspy breath before I'm taken away.

She's done it. She's outwitted me. She knew I'd go for it … and I knew it, too … and yet I did it anyway.

CHAPTER 11

VANESSA

The next day …

In the police station, I stare at the wall, drinking water from a plastic cup, thinking about Phoenix. He's been on my mind for ages … ever since I saw him at the party … the moment I knew he was back in my life.

Yes, I've known Phoenix longer than just a few days. Longer than weeks … months … even years. Our history goes way back, except back then he wasn't a ruthless killer going under the name Phoenix Sullivan, and I wasn't the coldhearted bitch that I am today.

When I said he was a stranger, I meant it. I don't know him the way I used to, and neither does he know me for how I am today. However, I have a feeling this is far from over.

Even though he is in a cell right now, it only takes one moment for him to escape. Now that I've seen what he's capable of, I know this is just the beginning of the end.

It didn't always used to be like this. There was a time when he was just as innocent as I portray myself to be. But like everything else in this world, we changed as time passed, and so did our personalities ... our appearance... our goals.

When I saw Phoenix at the party, I knew he was a changed man. I didn't know to what extent, but it didn't matter to me. I was still attracted to him ... like I've always been. We're like magnets, two opposing forces clashing with each other again and again.

Only this time I came out on top.

The police found the girl's body in the sand, and ultimately traced it back to his apartment, where conveniently the poison that also killed my husband was found, stashed underneath the couch. Put one and two together, and you have a murder case solved.

My name was cleared, even though one might argue that I'm sleeping with my husband's brother and had therefore planned everything with him in order to get rid of Phillip. However, it turns out the case of the curious killer, aka Phoenix Sullivan, is a much more believable plot. Especially when combined with photos that I took of my husband with his girlfriend. His motive became unquestionable.

How fortunate for me.

But here's the truth: I'm as much conniving as this supposed killer.

One could argue who of us two is the real killer.

I guess things like that will always stay inconclusive.

As I walk through the hallway of the police station, still drinking my water, I take a peek through one of the interrogation room windows; the one Phoenix is in. And for a moment, he gazes into my eyes, which are filled with delight upon seeing his hands chained to the table. He screams, "Vanessa! I'm going to kill you for this!"

Smiling at him, I wink and blow him a kiss. Then I turn around. Throwing my plastic cup in the bin, I can't help but think 'let him try.'

CHAPTER 12

VANESSA

Yesterday, before the arrest

"Pablo, I'm going out. Lock the windows for me, will you? And don't let anyone in unless it's me," I say as I put on my white gloves.

"Do you need a lift, madam?" he asks as he watches me put on my coat.

"No, thank you. I'd rather go alone." The truth is that I don't want anyone snooping around while I'm hunting for a killer.

Time to pay Phoenix Sullivan a visit. I'm going in broad daylight because I assume he won't be home during the day and probably doesn't expect me to come at this time. Always surprise your enemies.

I jump in my Aston Martin convertible and drive

off, putting the address into my TomTom as I race through the streets. I'm just below the speed limit, so I won't get a ticket but still able to get to his house quick.

When I get there, it's not at all what I expected. A small apartment building in the middle of town, with noisy cars racing by, streetlights shining through the windows that probably keep the tenants awake, and an awfully rotten smell hanging in the air. Damn, I didn't know killers could live like this. Well, the more you know…

I park my car somewhere hidden from the apartment building and then make my way to the front door. Before I go in, I check if there's anyone following me or looking at me. When I know the coast is clear, I enter the building and go up the stairs.

Number fifteen is just above, and the closer I get, the harder my heart is beating. I'm starting to wonder if he's really not home. I mean, would killers kill in broad daylight? Maybe not. Maybe he's home, waiting for me so he can strike me down where I'm vulnerable … in his own home. I'm walking into my own grave.

Except, the moment I realize this could all go to hell, I've already knocked on the door.

I wanted to make sure nobody was home.

What a stupid move.

I want to slap myself in the face for even considering it, but now it's too late. The handle is moving, the lock fiddled with, and then the creaky door opens. I swallow away the fear seeping down my throat, which feels blocked as I face the person who steps forward.

It's a woman.

Confused, I part my lips, but I have no idea what to say. I wasn't expecting anyone to be in here, let alone a woman. I'm a bit flabbergasted.

"Hi, can I help you?" she asks.

Frowning, I gaze at her. She looks so familiar, but I don't know why.

"Uh …" I briefly shake my head to pull myself together. "I'm sorry, I'm a bit confused. I thought a guy named Phoenix lived here?"

"Yeah, he does, but he isn't here right now." The door closes a little, and I get the sense that she isn't so keen on actually helping at all.

I place my hand on the door. "Wait."

She looks up at me with frightened doe-like eyes, her fingers clutching around the wood in an attempt to brace herself for what's coming. And that's when I realize why she looks so familiar. Those eyes, that voice, the way she moves … My jaw drops.

"It's you …" I mumble. "You live in his house … You're Phoenix's girlfriend?"

She looks confused. "Yes, but please leave now."

Oh, my god. I can't believe it.

Phoenix's girlfriend is the same woman who slept with my husband.

Within a second, my gloved hands are around her throat as I push her inside and slam the door shut with my heel. No one needs to see or hear what's going to happen in here.

***

PHOENIX

With a nice cash withdrawal, I make my way back to the car, ensuring I've tucked the money safely in my bag. I throw it in the backseat of the car and drive off. It's not much, but it's more than any man normally carries, which is why I'm careful not to run into any police by driving cautiously.

My girl doesn't know about this money. She thinks I'm a poor salesman, and I'd rather keep it that way. Fuck, if she knew I was carrying this much cash, she'd try to pry it from my fingers. She'd probably even go as far as to rake it from underneath my dead body, that money hungry bitch.

Nope, no way I'm ever going to tell her what I really do for a living. Besides, it's too complicated and too many things at once. I'm what you call a jack-of-all-trades. If they want me to kill, I kill. If they want me to sell drugs or torture someone, I will do just that. I don't care what or where, I will get the job done, which is why people like to pay me.

Don't judge me. I do what I must to survive.

Besides, it's not like I'm the only one with a questionable profession. My girl isn't a saint, either. She works at a strip club where customers love to take pictures of the women, including mine. I don't mind, it's not like they're competition anyway.

Unless, of course, she tries to fuck them. In which case, I will bury them alive.

Don't fucking touch my girl. I don't love her, hell, I don't even fucking like the bitch, but her pussy is mine and no other man will get between those legs. Ever. Which is also one of the reasons Phillip Starr is now dead.

I park my car close to the building and go up to my apartment. When I reach number fifteen, the door is open.

"What the …"

I tread carefully through the door, trying not to make a sound. I don't know what the fuck happened here, but I sure as hell won't be caught by surprise by some burglar. The curtains are closed and the lights are off, which turned the living room dark. I find the light switch and flip it on.

What I find in the middle of the room shocks me so much that I throw my keys so hard they make a hole in the wall.

"Fucking hell!"

My girl is tied up in a chair, her head hanging, showing no sign of life. I rush to her side and press a finger against her neck. No pulse.

"Fuck!" I fish in my pocket and take out the Swiss Knife I always carry with me and cut through the ropes that bind her, which turn out to be the ropes that kept the curtains together. I grab her lifeless body and place it on the ground. That's when I notice the foam bubbling out of her mouth.

"Oh, fuck no …" I mumble, pressing my hands on her chest.

I start pumping, using both hands to push down on her ribs. However, nothing seems to jumpstart her heart. After a few minutes, I give up and sit down with my head resting on the chair, sweat drops dripping down my back. Panting, I throw the knife on the floor and growl.

She's gone. I might not have loved her, but she lived with me for quite a few weeks, and I did actually enjoy her presence, unlike most women I spend time with. I can't believe she's gone. I might actually miss her. I didn't want her to die. It wasn't her time yet. Someone killed her, and it wasn't me.

Fuck that. I know who it was and what it was. She was poisoned, and from the smell of it, I know exactly where it was taken from.

I get up from the floor and search through the cabinets in my kitchen, throwing aside all other herb pots. I don't even care that they break apart on the floor, leaving a mess, as I fly through the cabinets looking for that one fucking bottle. The same bottle I used on Phillip Starr.

That one bottle is now gone.

And I know exactly who took it.

I know she saw my license plate, but fuck, I didn't think she'd actually go for it. I thought I scared her enough. Guess I was wrong. *Fuck!* I fucking hate her. She fucking dared to step foot into my house and murder my girlfriend? She'll fucking pay for this. I'll make sure of it.

Rage boils up inside me, consuming me whole, as I roar out loud. "Vanessa!"

CHAPTER 13

VANESSA

A few days later

The toaster dings, and I take out the toast and pour coffee into the mug, then bring it to Arthur on a tray. "Here you go, honey."

"Thank you," he says, smiling broadly like the lucky fucker he is. Finally, someone who's grateful for everything I do. Arthur is just the man I need in my life. Trustworthy, reliable, and humble. Not the type of man I usually go for, but it's certainly a breath of fresh air.

I go outside and get the mail from the mailbox. Inside, while drinking a cup of tea, I open the letters.

"Oh, look!" I say, holding up the one I'm reading. "It's from my lawyer."

"What's it about?" he asks.

"They're finally allowing me access to Phillip's funds."

His jaw drops. "Does that mean ..."

"Everything is mine!" I say, smiling. I'm so happy; I could burst into tears.

"Now you can invest it in your study. Your business. Maybe even your acting career," he says.

"I know, right? Finally ... it's time for *me*," I say, wiping away a tear while Arthur gets up from his seat.

"I'm so happy for you," he says, as he hugs me tight.

I'm still smiling like crazy as I open the next letter, but this one instantly wipes the smile off my face and punches me in the stomach as well. My hands shake as I read the words out loud.

I'll come for you, Princess. One way or another, I'm going to get you ... and when I do, be ready to run hard and fast.

Because I know what you've done.

~~Love~~ I hate you to death,

Phoenix

The end …
Or is it?

Flip the page!

STALKER

THE STANDALONE

Stalker is the Standalone connected to Killer. It follows Phoenix & Vanessa's story as they clash over love and hatred for the final time. Stalker is published on June 16th, 2015. You can find more information on my website: www.clarissawild.blogspot.com. Make sure you check it out!

Thank you so much for reading Killer, and I'll hope you continue with Stalker to complete the journey.

For updates about Stalker, please visit my website, www.clarissawild.blogspot.com or sign up for my newsletter here: http://eepurl.com/FdY71

I'd love to talk to you! You can find me on Facebook: facebook.com/ClarissaWildAuthor, make sure to click LIKE. You can also join the Fan Club: facebook.com/groups/FanClubClarissaWild/ and talk with other readers!

Enjoyed this book? You could really help out by leaving a review on Amazon and Goodreads. Thank you!

SUBSCRIBE TO CLARISSA'S NEWSLETTER

To receive exclusive updates from Clarissa Wild and to be the first to get your hands on her books, please sign up to be on her personal mailing list!

You'll get instant access to cover releases, chapter previews, free short stories, and you'll be eligible to win great prizes!

Link: http://eepurl.com/FdY71

Connect with Clarissa!

Website: www.clarissawild.blogspot.com
Twitter: www.twitter.com/WildClarissa
Facebook: www.facebook.com/ClarissaWildAuthor
Pinterest: www.pinterest.com/clarissawild
Google+: www.plus.google.com/+ClarissaWild

ALSO BY CLARISSA WILD

Dark Romance

Mr. X

Delirious Series

Killer

Stalker

New Adult Romance

Fierce Series

Blissful Series

Erotic Romance

The Billionaire's Bet Series

Enflamed Series

Visit Clarissa Wild's website for current titles.
http://clarissawild.blogspot.com

ABOUT THE AUTHOR

Clarissa Wild is the USA Today Bestselling author of FIERCE, a college romance series. She is also a writer of erotic romance such as the Blissful Series, The Billionaire's Bet series, the Doing It Series and the Enflamed Series. She is an avid reader and writer of sexy stories about hot men and feisty women. Her other loves include her furry cat friend and learning about different cultures. In her free time she enjoys watching all sorts of movies, reading tons of books and cooking her favorite meals.

Want to be informed of new releases and special offers? Sign up for Clarissa Wild's newsletter on her website clarissawild.blogspot.com.

Visit Clarissa Wild on Amazon for current titles.

Made in the USA
Monee, IL
05 March 2025

13551056R00080